WILLIAM M. BRANDON III

SPACEBOY BOOKS

Denver, Colorado

Published in the United States by:
Spaceboy Books LLC
1627 Vine Street
Denver, CO 80206
www.readspaceboy.com

First printed July 2020

ISBN: 978-1-951393-03-8

Praise for *Welcome to Spring Street*:

"Brandon takes us into an alternative version of our own world with the confidence and resolve of a well-worn psychic-voyager. Multi-layered, multi-stylized, and featuring a wild and diverse cast, *Welcome to Spring Street* is a spark of hopeful art against authority and those who abuse power. Read this wisely!"

— Jordan A. Rothacker, author of *Gristle: weird tales* and the forthcoming, *The Death of the Cyborg Oracle*

"William M. Brandon III has a vision that cuts to the core of where we are now and shines a light on the forces of the underground. Moving from downtown Los Angeles's dive bars to the memory of Occupy encampments and beyond, *Welcome to Spring Street* is a pulsing ride through corruption, insurgency, and, ultimately, hope."

— Saskia Vogel, author of *Permission*

"*Welcome to Spring Street* is a portrait of a Los Angeles that once seemed fictional, but becomes less so every time I read it. Brandon's ensemble cast foretells a brutal future, one that increasingly feels like it is arriving eerily close to *Spring Street's* schedule. Is there a way out? Is there a safe place? *Spring Street* has no easy answers, only the cold comfort of its Noir world that lingers even after you put the book down."

— Scott Gilbertson, *WIRED*

"If Bukowski wrote about anarchists, dissidents, and reactionaries, the result would be *Welcome to Spring Street*. A prescient and delightfully discombobulating take on the American police state."

— Jim Ruland, author of *DO WHAT YOU WANT: The Story of Bad Religion*

for
René Claire
Quentin Ryan
Greyson René
In hopes that they create a
better world
than we left for them

Send William a postcard or letter, he always writes back
PO Box #325
Athens, GA 30603

11/30/~~2011~~ NM11
(Dis) Honorable A. Villaraicossa
Mayor of Los Angeles
200 N. Main St. Rm. 103
LA, CA 90012

RE: THE FORCED EVICTION OF PEACEFUL
    PROTESTERS FROM CITY HALL

The People know that you are a liar, a coward,
and a pathetic excuse for a leader. Now, the
whole world knows.

If you had a sliver of integrity, you would
resign. You represent everything that is wrong
with Los Angeles and America.

with utter disgust,
Kuras Arius
548 Spring St.
LA, CA 90013

We live in the darkness, just before dawn.

SUMMER NM13
WEDNESDAY

01

Tonight, Keagan was free to drink under the polluted downtown moon. The past three days in a dim underground apartment had been an improvement, he'd already spent three months crushed in a Nevada drone hanger with two hundred people. The Revision of Origin Program kept Keagan quarantined when he arrived in Los Angeles, but tonight he walked through the lobby of the Spring Street Lofts, a free man.

To the south, Spring Street was choked with coffee-shop philosophers and celebrity trainwrecks. To the north were badlands; the knives of gentrification had not yet prevailed. Below Main Street, Keagan caught sight of two men drunkenly snapping out a tired but heartfelt rendition of *Georgia on My Mind*. Above their heads, an ancient hand-painted sign read *King Eddy's Saloon*. Large power boxes fixed to the corner of the century-old King Edward Hotel bore stenciled *LAPD* insignia and an imperious warning that the LAPD was, at all times, monitoring the entire intersection via live-feed video.

King Eddy's was a brightly lit room with a large four-sided bar, behind which a weatherworn man by the name of Popeye served beer to a row of indigent old timers. A minor contingent of addled twenty-somethings slithered about, waiting until an angle for a free beverage presented itself.

Keagan chose to sit next to a kindly older gentleman dressed head to toe in West Texas-cowboy business-casual. He seemed harmless by comparison.

Keagan muttered as he took his seat. "Beer please. Dark, if you have it."

Popeye flipped his dentures once and winked at Keagan.

Keagan tried not to look shocked.

"Makes me sick." The cowboy muttered into his beer.

"Wow, ok, I didn't know if I was the only one who saw that. Doesn't seem right..."

"Of course it ain't right!" The Cowboy got flustered fast. "Jesus kid, what planet are you from?"

"I must have misunderstood..."

"Parking meter attendants, goddamn it. Motherfucking Gestapo sons of whores, riding around in their tiny little clown cars ruinin' perfectly good sunny days."

"Sure, they are a menace, no argument here."

"We take care of it, where I'm from."

"Oh yeah?" Keagan received his beer and scanned the room for a less volatile bar mate.

"Shoot 'em in the fucking eye."

"What?"

"That's right, I don't give a fuck if it's a lady. One shot, right in the eye, so they know it's us."

"Okay. Well, that was really---" Keagan turned to leave.

The Cowboy grabbed his arm, "My buddies and I, we're in oil, ya see? Oil and guns. I like to come out here and dry out a little; Texas gets a bit damp, especially in the summer."

"I lived in San Antonio for a while..."

"San Antonio? No shit, you're a Texan?" The Cowboy looked Keagan up and down.

"No sir, I was born in Nevada."

"Ah. You don't look like a Texan...so you see, we all got sick of subsidizing the City's income so we put bounties on their heads. We put two or three million, depending on how many foreign wars are going full steam. Sometimes we get creative. Do you 'member, ten years back, there was a young man walked into a grocery store and systematically kill't four customers with a ninja sword?"

4

"I didn't live here yet..."

"Two of the casualties were bounty hits. It was absolute genius." The cowboy laughed slowly.

Keagan looked across the bar and stopped dead on a young woman running her hand across her throat in a cutting motion. Keagan smiled, and took the hint.

"Pleased to meet you. Take care."

"Wait," The Cowboy called after him, "I ain't told you about tonight's bounty."

Keagan sat next to the kind woman. "Thank you, I feel certain that any further conversation between that gentleman and myself would turn out poorly."

"Don't mention it. He's just one of the many magical headcases that make King Eddy's so homey. You should see how jumpin' the place gets when the Twin Towers bus drops off."

"Twin Towers?"

"The prison. What planet are you from?"

"A small and desolate planet called Las Vegas. Our people are friendly toward your people..."

"Great, another smart ass. Do you live upstairs?"

"No, I live on Sixth and Spring, the SS Lofts."

"Same here." Her eyes displayed a polite apathy. "Don't call it that."

"SS? I thought it was kind of funny..."

"*Lofts*, don't call it *Lofts*. It's bad enough that they're letting greedy developers gut these old buildings, we don't have to play along in the newspeak."

"Seems like a good thing to me, but I just got here, so-"

"Exactly. You just got here." The young woman faced Keagan and smiled. "I'm Glad you said no."

"No?"

"To living upstairs." The woman gestured toward the ceiling. "I keep my conversations short with people who live in this dump."

"I'm glad to be less repellant."

"That's an awful fancy outfit for Skid Row." She pointed to Keagan's suit.

"I guess it is. I feel most comfortable in a suit. Hey, at least I've loosened my tie to signify casual post-work relaxation."

The woman glanced at his purposely-disheveled necktie and collar button, "You certainly have a way with words."

Keagan blushed. "That's not all I have a way with."

"Wrong answer." The woman began to gather her bottle and cigarettes.

"Wait, I'm sorry, I'm not trying to hit on you. I was flattered, probably didn't handle it well."

"Strike one is past us now. Try to mind the baselines."

Keagan couldn't tell if she was under or overdressed. Her antique shirt once inspired pride, but its straight lines had been marred naively by emergency surgery. Hems along the neckline shortened its life uncomfortably—making ragged what was once whole.

"Let's get back to you, asshole. Why are you drinking from a dirty glass in His Highness' Saloon?"

"I needed to get out."

"Please elaborate." The woman eyed Keagan as he adjusted his tie.

"I have a book to write, but I have a problem with my pages disappearing, usually late at night, and typically after a nice writing jag. I had a good day today, page-count-wise, and decided to drink myself to sleep."

"What floor are you on?"

"Basement."

"The basement? I thought they stopped renting rooms down there."

"I'm special." Keagan smirked.

"Great, I can't wait to hear."

"I negotiated a quick turn around Revision so that I could finish my book in LA."

"You're in the Revision program." The woman looked into the distance, considering her words. "How long have they kept you down there?"

"Three days. Three long days. They said Program members sometimes transfer to higher floors, but lucky me, I'm down there all by myself. Well, as far as I can tell. I hear *things* sometimes. Kind of creepy."

"No one's lived down there for years, if that helps. Only rumors survive about the last tenants," the woman offered.

"My name is Keagan by the way, Seward Keagan."

"Cadence," she extended her hand.

"When I first moved in I heard music, conversations, and a little fornication filtering down through the thick concrete slab above my head. The joys and sorrows of thirteen floors escaped opening elevator doors and bounced along those rough, unfinished basement corridors. When typing would not drown out the noise, I resigned to bear witness. Then, I heard *it*."

"It?" Cadence crinkled up her nose.

"Something very, *very* heavy was dropped, the floor heaved and then the silence returned."

"Okay, that is weird."

"So I decided to investigate. I walked the gnarled ring of corridors but found nothing. I made a second lap, holding my ear to every apartment door, and I heard nothing. Absolutely nothing."

"Could have been the subway running past, small earthquake, or maybe a..."

"No, something was dropped. That's not all..."

Cadence leaned in.

"One night, I heard conversation and quiet music, very quiet and very clear. So clear that I could tell it wasn't coming through the building. I ran into the hallway, following the twisted walls and the sickly sweet treble of late seventies punk. Then it stopped. As if I had tripped an alarm, or someone had heard my footfalls. I tried several doors, all were locked, and then one, B-03, opened." Cadence looked away. "I walked into the apartment and the stench of freshly crushed cigarettes and cheap lager hung in the air for just a moment before evaporating."

"Squatters?" Cadence asked.

"Maybe. There were no furnishings, but the place was immaculately clean, had been immaculately *cleaned*, I mean, and recently."

"But the apartment was empty?"

"Even the cupboards in the bathroom."

"Weird."

"Someone was there."

"Yes, and then they walked through the wall until the coast was clear, eh?"

"Something like that." Keagan had felt the heat of congregation.

"Don't go koo-koo bird down in that basement okay? You seem like a decent kid and I'd hate to read about you jumping off the building because the *voices in the basement* told you to." For the first time Cadence took notice of Keagan's angular, clean-shaven face. His long Roman nose hooked when he smiled, and his light, distracted eyes reminded her of Orin.

Cadence kicked Keagan's stool with the steel toe of her boot, "So are the ghosts stealing your writing?"

"I'm afraid that the problem is a bit more delicate."

02

Kuraš was alone. When he woke in the morning, he woke to a large empty room, in a chair fit for one. Kuraš owned one set of dishes, one pen, and one lighter—a gunmetal wick lighter with *ATHEIST* ground into one side of the case.

Only his estranged daughter remained in sporadic, patient contact. Shannon was exhausted by her biological father's constant need to be right. He simply could not let things go. Right or wrong, Kuraš knew a little too much about a little too much and when he got started, he kept filling in blanks long after the conversation ended.

By the time the coddled tenants of the Spring Street Lofts began to wake and prepare for school and vocation, Kuraš had devoured an entire news cycle and retired to the roof to watch grey, soot-encased, Los Angeles shine beneath pale veins of morning light.

What a waste, Kuraš lamented. The business-savvy fixie-bike-kids and their practiced air of Nihilism brought a new and unwelcome attitude to Spring Street. These entitled swine slipped from adolescence into adulthood managing only to burden the world with their haphazard and narcissistic *art*. Their apathy toward the society crumbling around them scared Kuraš.

"Hello?" Kuraš' daughter sounded impatient; the children were running amok.

"Hi there Shannon, it's your Dad." His smile beamed through the phone line.

"Oh. Hello, Kuraš. What do you need?"

She forgot their appointment.

"We had an…"

Shannon covered the phone's mouthpiece and shouted, "Hey, put that down…put it down now!"

"It sounds like a bad time. I'll try again soon." Kuraš offered, like a whipped hound.

Shannon paused. "Okay. If you must…"

Kuraš hung up the phone.

It was the last time he tried to call her.

03

"Incredulous." Will added from behind a long sketchpad.

"No, I don't think that works, she's not *unwilling* to believe, or *incapable* of believing, she's just *skeptical.*" Liam pressed his finely manicured hair against his scalp and set his short-brimmed fedora on the bar. In the diminished light his suit looked like grey tweed and his vest a pale green silk; he was greatly put-off.

"Skeptical? A third-grader?" Will asked pointedly.

"Yeeees." Liam answered slowly.

"Okay? Well, I don't recall being a particularly skeptical third grader." Will didn't remember much about third grade past building forts, and riding his bike from one side of the neighborhood to the next.

"Really? Third grade was a time of great skepticism for me."

"How so?"

"Just a lot of boundary pushing. The Santa thing went bust for me almost right away. Jesus followed shortly after."

"Yeah?"

"Sure, it was logic. For instance- my family moved a lot, yet the Jolly One always had a forwarding address. We never had a chimney, yet Santa had a flawless B&E record. We lived in the South, so you lose a bit of the snow/tree wonderment, and the sleigh becomes a liability, right?"

Will laughed heartily, "Right. Santa in Daisy Dukes."

"Anyway, calling bullshit on ol' Santa made Jesus the next on the chopping block. They're basically the same archetype to a child."

"So you just went along?"

"No, I formally requested absolution from both ex-mas and church. My parents wedged me into a compromise; I attended church with my parents until my eighteenth birthday and was required to be respectful, but never to pay lip service or pretend. My parents were American Baptists, so ritual was virtually non-existent, and all religious experience could be put-off as subjective and deeply internal."

"You must have been a real joy to your parents." Will added.

"In some ways. I was never a cowed or overwhelmed child, and could hold my own in the company of adults."

"That makes sense. You've always been an ass-kisser."

Liam bowed, "A *professional* ass-kisser. I'm not sure why my considerable talents are being squandered on this project. No offense."

"None taken. I heard you were a pain in the ass narcissist."

"What? Who would say such a thing?"

"You're on this project because you pissed off the right people. If you were a precious talent, they'd never let you anywhere near me."

"I see." Liam was wounded.

"So, we have a skeptical third grader who is on the verge of breaking this whole Santa BS open with a few finely placed image-bombs distributed to unsuspecting children."

"Yes, children who are singing in the ex-mas eve choir at *Whatever Town* Pentecostal Church."

"Literal confetti bombs, set to go off and blow the lid on ex-mas." Will was sketching a child's surprised expression amid a sea of innocent singing faces.

"The image bombs, they contain a lynchpin secret, a refutation that will immediately effect all children simultaneously."

"Santa shaving his back hair?" Will offered.

"Mrs. Claus shaving his back hair." Liam countered.

"Pictures...pictures..." Will staved off laughter, searching for the right image.

"Of their parents putting gifts under the tree."

"Not Santa." Will added.

"Exactly." Liam smiled.

"Curlers, robes, underpants, high-balls, joints, thongs..."

"Children's book, Will. Focus." Liam placed his hand on Will's shoulder.

04

Jean-Baptisté Baudron and Lara Connor were perfect. Perfect people, perfect bodies, perfect for one another. They were both born at six-fifteen, postmeridian. Jean-Baptisté in sunny, uncaring San Diego, California and Lara in oppressive Toccopola, Mississippi.

Lara's parents were heavy-handed Jehovah's Witnesses, with a minor hat tip to the Manson concept of *family*. Her father, mother, and seven siblings, were scam artists: short-run employment scams, worker's comp, harassment, et cetera. When the governments of Florida, Mississippi, and both Carolinas got wise to their interstate antics, the Connors fled to Riverside County, California, and hid among the post-war suburbs and dilapidated trailer parks.

Lara's beauty, even as an infant, bent gazes, and turned heads. The Connor parents were con-artist-attractive, but their youngest daughter made man, woman, and child stop and forget their wallet, purse, necklace, or watch. The Connors made Lara the main attraction, and spent the rest of their days picking pockets at the local mall.

When Mr. and Mrs. Connor passed, the underage siblings buried them in a shallow grave out back and pretended nothing had changed. Lara remained the star of the show, but as her drive to remain hidden intensified, her charismatic beauty was soured by wrath. Without a stake in the family business, Lara was banished to make her way, in whatever way a wrathful eleven year old can.

Jean-Baptisté was a superb athlete, and his parents took high-priced care to move him close to a nationally ranked private high school in Los Angeles. His father harbored a hope that Jean-Baptisté would become a professional football player, or perhaps medal in the Olympics. His mother, more pragmatic, wished him a stunning wife and a litter of brilliant doe-eyed children for her to fuss over.

An injury during a non-conference game shattered his father's dream. After fifteen pins from ankle to toes, Jean-Baptisté would run no more. It was apparent to all but his father that Jean-Baptisté would not go on to play professional sports. The despair created something bleak inside Mr. Baudron and he disappeared slowly into his law library with his prized canters of rare scotch.

Jean-Baptisté's mother took a hiatus from location filming overseas and tried to connect with her son during his time of need. Her sudden insistence on an intense mother-son bond drove Jean-Baptisté into a petulant solitude. In a week's time, She threw her hands up in martyrdom and was gone, as rapidly as she had arrived.

The boy fell into a rough, heavy-drinking crowd and was soon spending his weekends hunched over disemboweled automobiles with four (equally drunk) men. By the light of the moon, Jean Baptisté and the rest of the Creeps car club danced with girls in Victory Rolls, flowered dresses, and back-seamed stockings until two ante-meridian. Venomous vixens kept his ferocious sense of self-pity at bay, and the tattooed, beer-guzzling trainwrecks of Los Angeles County provided Jean-Baptisté with a perfect escape from his warped archetype of *family*.

§

The Creeps were blind-drunk and looking for a fight as they pulled up to Taxi's Bar on Main Street. They parked and polished off another flask of whiskey before stumbling in the bar's back door. A jump-jazz quartet lit the small stage up and Jean-Baptisté surveyed the dance floor.

Everyone was in uniform. The ladies in their (don't touch me) dresses and pristine (don't you dare touch me) makeup, stood silent and watchful as the lost Buddhas of Afghanistan. The men were a rhythmic sea of mediocrity: same suits, same hats, same jack-boot-bluejeanslickhaired cliché. Jean-Baptisté was ready to find someone to fawn over —at home.

Lara Connor was not wearing a dress, and her long black hair was tied up in a dirty red bandana when she dropped a twenty-two-ounce bottle of English ale. Jean-Baptisté spun and caught the bottle before the fine amber liquid was sacrificed to the pungent barroom floor. Lara's hands were at her cheeks, preparing to shriek in frustration, when She raised her emerald eyes to meet Jean-Baptisté's. Though her lipstick and eyeliner were pristine, her wifebeater and heavy jeans were slick with engine grime. It was lust at first sight.

They spent the evening enthralled with one another's every word and movement. She was lost in his careless face and fierce, strong hands, and he in her unrelenting beauty. Last call and the harsh house lights ruptured their insular universe.

"Looks like we have to split." He smiled.

"It does."

"May I walk you to your car?"

"You may," Lara smiled.

The couple left the bar and sauntered into the night air. They kept an intense minimal distance between their bodies as they walked, as if a single touch would throw them both into the abyss. When they reached her vehicle he closed the gap between them. Lara moved toward Jean-Baptisté and he met her ascent—resting his hand on the small of her arched back and lifting her to his strong but submissive lips.

Jean-Baptisté rummaged through his pocket; in a flash he scribbled his phone number on Lara's wrist.

Instead of laying wagers on the couple's potential for committing to nuptials, people placed solid money on how long it would take for the twin supernovas to collapse and coalesce into a galaxy all their own.

Three months. That's how long. The couple announced their engagement and eloped within the hour. They chose a Justice of the Peace, and two witnesses—state provided. Jean-Baptisté and Lara were one.

In the calm honeymoon dusk, Lara emerged from a scalding shower and Jean-Baptisté wrapped her in his arms. Her body opened to him uninhibited and their vicious assault cracked the medicine cabinet and sacrificed a candleholder to the soft white tundra of a clawfoot bathtub.

So it was that Lara and Jean-Baptisté destroyed whatever room they were left alone in. Were they given the time to dress and undress, they would. If only for a stolen moment, a silent, patient fuck, they would try.

Before long, they were soon no longer invited to acceptable social gatherings. The exiled lovers poured the last of their money into a cheap Hollywood apartment. Jean-Baptisté wanted to be a movie star. His parents could not understand why their son had *run off with trailer trash to live in filth and chase a fantasy. Why not go to law school and hedge those bets, son?* Mr. and Mrs. Baudron refused to assist in what they called *an enormous and vile mistake, a clichéd waste of a potentially important life.*

As winter passed, Jean-Baptisté labored in the puppy-mill of bit-part auditions, while holding down a full-time job as a machinist. His faithful companion helped make ends meet with two part-time jobs. Their Herculean love began to fray at the frustrated and rejected edges and their devotion became more desperate and contrived.

§

The summer sun sank into the ocean while Best Coast Ray sneered, "Sweetheart, he's a looker, there's no doubt, but so are you. I want you more than I want him."

"But I'm not a model." Lara pleaded.

"Neither is he."

"Women and men alike fall all over him. The truth is, he can't act. Okay, it's worse than that, it's painful to watch him try. But look at the stills, he is incapable of taking a bad picture."

"Look gorgeous, I'm in the big time now. When I say someone is a star, my reputation is on the line. I need better incentive than *people want to fuck him.*"

Lara clenched her white-gloved hands out of Ray's view. Her powder, hair, skirt, stockings, blouse, and blood-red lipstick were intentional. She should never have come to him.

"I need you to be part of the deal somehow." Ray insisted.

"Maybe." Lara prepared herself for the worst.

"You're like a unicorn from my distant past, lovely Lara." Ray stood and walked around his lightboard to Lara's shoulder. "I need proof of your existence." Lara stared forward in disciplined disdain. The room was suffocating; Ray cleared his throat, "One shoot, little lady. Just one. No publishing, no web-traffic, right here, right now, nude. Maybe some smoking---"

"No."

"I'll put Jenny-the-Baptist in Versace and Prada by week's end."

"His name is Jean-Baptisté," Lara kept her composure. "If you touch me, I'll slice your belly open and play around in your guts."

"Just like old times lovely Lara, just like old times."

When Best Coast Ray met Jean-Baptisté he flushed red and found his seat with both hands, unable to take his gaze from Jean-Baptisté's sunlight bathed eyes. "Please have a seat, young man."

Lara smiled. Ray had not looked in her direction, he simply leered embarrassingly at Jean-Baptisté. "So Ray, do we have a deal?"

"Oh yes. Yes, we most certainly have a deal."

Ray had no trouble living up to his word. Promoting Jean-Baptisté was effortless. He had no 'talent' for modeling per se, but he was, alarmingly and enduringly photogenic. For the most part, wardrobe and setting comprised the complete nightmare of a shoot with Jean-Baptisté. He was always impeccable, through no effort of his own.

The lovebirds fled from their dingy Hollywood nest, and perched in quiet solitude high above formerly surly Spring Street, as trendy downtown pioneers. They whiled away their hours in one another's embrace, spending as little time apart as their lives would allow.

THURSDAY

05

Keagan lifted a bulging file folder from his makeshift desk. As he began to examine the contents his phone alarm sounded. "Shit, I'm going to be late." Keagan slipped the folder under his arm and locked his door. Low, dark clouds forecast a storm. On any other day Keagan's wee black heart would have leapt with joy at the hint of rain, but today he faced public transportation with an unkempt stack of absorbent, typewritten manuscript pages that were irreplaceable. Keagan tipped his felt fedora forward and smothered the chaotic stack of papers beneath his black wool overcoat.

A nettlesome sun pressed through weak fissures in the clouds and bathed north Spring Street in temporary quicksilver. The mid-morning sidewalks were rife with yoga pants, designer hound dogs, and sleepwalkers sipping seven-dollar cups of cheaply pungent Arabica. The occasional blindly drunk and/or indigent passerby broke the cacophonous banality.

The Biltmore Millennium loomed domineeringly over Pershing Square, just beneath a low ceiling of grey that swallowed the skyscrapers of the financial district. Keagan boarded a Purple Line train, took a seat, and rode alone beneath Macarthur Park.

Keagan opened his flimsy folder to perform a cursory review of his work. As he scanned, he discovered a hand-written note about the schedule of psychological development being used as a plotline. He was confused, but pulled the note out and set it on the seat next to him. A few pages later, he found another intruder. This time, an xmas card from his mom, at least two or three years old. Soon, he could not amass ten pages without an insert: a menu for Gill's in the Stillwell Hotel, 2010 1099 filing instructions (in toto), a typewritten letter to an old friend Keagan had tried hard to forget, and finally the bulk of an unfinished manuscript from a decade prior—the 'white whale' manuscript.

Keagan placed his foot on the seat in front of him. A disembodied voice recited, "Please take your feet off of the seat sir. It is against regulation *crackle* 1649 (c) of the Municipal code for *crackle* *sputter* —silence.

These people don't miss a beat. Keagan placed his foot on the floor beneath his hard plastic seat. He kept removing the non-sequitur articles one by one until he was left with a paltry fifty-five pages.

The disappearing pages started in the basement. In the dark, amidst the deafening calm, he folded a sheet of typewritten paper, rending it twice. The heavy cotton tore quietly; it was no relief. He kept tearing, but only gained smaller pieces. Keagan placed a small slip of paper in his mouth, he did not know why, and kneaded the pulp with his tongue. And then again.

Keagan felt sick to his stomach. It had to stop; he had to figure out a way to stop it. The missing pages represented two month's work, possibly his best, or most dismal offerings. He would never know.

Keagan rode west on the tilting 20 bus with a dull ache in his head and a woefully inadequate list of excuses for failing his publisher's benchmark. It was the sort of thing that modern day publishers (read: corporate CEOs) associated with lost profits and diminished executive bonuses. He would lose his deal if he didn't wrest control over his urges. Off to Revision again, deported to Nevada for certain.

As he scolded himself, even as he begged himself to heed the symptoms, Keagan tenderly fingered a typewritten page—folded in fourths, and placed unconsciously in the breast pocket of his shirt for the long ride home.

The 20 bus skidded to a perilous halt and Keagan leaped from the door over a grey rushing river. The rain came. Wilshire was dark and sullen.

Fifty-Seven-Fifty Wilshire was a hulking brick-colored professional-office-resort replete with imported trees, grinning, lobotomized security personnel, and wide expanses of darkly tinted corner offices surrounding bays of cubicle-shaped human pens.

The security guard said hello to Keagan and then did a double take. "Sir," he called after Keagan, "Sir, who are you here to see?"

"This is your mom's address isn't it?" Keagan asked rapidly.

"What?"

"I'm here to see Samuel Irvine."

"Is he expecting you?"

"No, I felt like wasting my day dropping by."

The security officer returned to his desk to call the SI Publishing office. Keagan ducked into the stairwell while he was distracted and took the stairs, two at a time, to SI Publishing International.

The lobby was long and immense, Keagan waved at the receptionist seated at a desk on the far side. The walls, flooring, and furniture had been molested by a coven of ex-boutique-hotel-interior-designers. Dark, lacquered branches crawled the space like satanic kudzu, and were backlit by walls composed of nauseating white light. Immense, cackling water installations lined both walls and added an unpleasant patina of corrosion to the sparkling, brand new interior.

"Mr. Keagan," the receptionist's voice was projected by some trick of acoustics, or hidden speaker, "Mr. Irvine's representative is waiting for you." The receptionist raised a limp arm and pointed beyond the desk.

The receptionist had ingested at least eight Xanax in the past twenty-four hours, and her lips whispered between words. Her eyes were lidded—*bedroom eyes* they were called back when Heroin was a chic way to cure headaches. She stood and led Keagan into a long hallway before seating him in a large office overlooking the south of Los Angeles from behind enormous tinted windows.

"Jason will be with you shortly."

"Thank you," Keagan called over his shoulder, but she had already closed the door behind her.

Keagan waited impatiently in the large office. The furniture was from someone's vision of a Man-Cave, as were the magazines strewn on the low glass coffee table, and the cheap faux-modern desk.

A slim man popped into the office like a tardy uncle at the birthday party.

"Seward Keagan! Boy is it a pleasure, an honor really, to finally meet you Mr. Keagan."

Keagan was flattered; the representative they sent him was good enough to afford three thousand dollar suits and weekly haircuts. He stood and shook the rep's hand, he was all gleaming porcelain caps and thick, sculpted hair. The rep throttled Keagan's arm with the enthusiasm of a desperate game show host.

"Jason?"

"Yes, that's right."

"Okay. Look, Jason, I have some bad news," Keagan watched Jason walk behind the large desk and sit attentively in the faux-leather chair. "I only have half of what I'm supposed to."

Jason's expression hardened and he leaned back in his seat. "Half? So...like...around one fifty?"

"Well, no. One hundred pages was what I was supposed to bring in, I have a little over fifty." Keagan answered weakly.

"Only supposed to be a hundred pages. Really? Are you sure about that?"

Ah fuck, here it comes "Yes, one-hundred. I had the pages, I've misplaced two large chunks I was working on this month, but I'll be able to re-type them from memory."

"Okay yes, that's good, let's do that. So I guess what I'm going to tell Mr. Irvine is that you didn't have what we requested."

"You could say that. You could also say that you were aware of them but had only reviewed a portion."

"Mr. Keagan, I don't think you understand how it works here..."

"Jason, I know precisely how it works, which is why I am asking for some wiggle room on this. The book, in case you are curious, is coming along very well. I solved the problem I had with the protagonist and his relationship with the...-"

"Yes, yes, that's good Mr. Keagan. Is that the manuscript?" Jason pointed to the stack of papers Keagan had placed in front of him.

"It is."

"May I?"

"Of course."

The rep made Keagan suffer; he would not dismiss him. He pulled one page at a time from the stack and read the collection of pieces in its entirety.

"Mr. Keagan, I don't know what to say, I am intrigued and a bit dumbfounded."

"Thank you Jason."

"This is the thing Seward, may I call you Seward? The thing is, I need that three hundred pages. I can stall for another week, but if I can't put those pages in front of Mr. Irvine next Wednesday, I'll be looking for another job, in another industry. And so will you."

"Understood, Jason."

"I hope to see you again soon Mr. Keagan, thank you for coming all the way down in the rain. By the way, there are only forty-five pages here." Jason stood and reached for Keagan's hand.

Keagan returned the shake, wary from the last time, "Thanks Jason, could have sworn there were fifty."

Keagan left the decadent publishing office, scolded, and rightly anxious about the next visit. Three hundred pages, *No excuses*. It would do no good for Keagan to explain that their shining star was devouring their profits nightly.

Keagan felt certain he had an additional eighty pages in a drawer near his mattress, but he couldn't be certain they were safe. When he opened his folder again, the disheveled pages that flapped between Keagan's frantic filing fingers had now dwindled to forty-two.

06

"Fuck them. I say we bomb the place smooth as glass and walk away." A young man, a victim of the *skinny-jeans* madness permeating LA fashion, snickered to his compatriot.

"What? Did I just hear you say, *bomb it smooth as glass*? Is that some sort of sand/Middle East joke?" Kuraš never looked at the kid; he didn't have to.

"Yeah, something like that gramps, mind your own business."

"This is my business son," Kuraš' eyes narrowed.

"Oh shit, here it comes." Josh/Mike turned his stool and the rest of the kids at the corner dive bar collected around Kuraš. The ragtag band of drunkards had known one another for precisely nine hundred seconds, but Josh/Mike gathered an audience like the Atlantic gathers rain. His slim, purposeful mustache and late-Victorian attire made him an attendant dandy on both sides of the Twentieth Century.

"Josh/Mike, back these fuckers off," Kuraš sneered.

"It's Joshua Michael, Kuraš. My name is Joshua Michael, *Joshua—Michael*," he explained to his motley band of paroled low-lives.

Kuraš leaned in and addressed the Skinny-Jeans Kid from an uncomfortable distance. "It's ignorant armchair commandos like you that get innocent people killed."

"Any crazy asshole looking to make nuclear warheads deserves a slap-down."

"Wow," Kuraš shook his head, "you are a really ignorant little lamb. Have you heard of the NPT?" Kuraš waited, the Skinny-Jeans Kid stared blankly. "The Nuclear Non-Proliferation Treaty was presented for signatures in nineteen sixty eight. Signatories agreed that all parties would: one, retard and eventually end proliferation, by destroying current stockpiles, two, honor each party's right to peaceful use of nuclear energy, and three, aid, invest in, and/or share technology with other signatory states wishing to use nuclear energy.

"The people you want to eviscerate from a safe height are signatories to that treaty, the US is a signatory, are you following me yet?"

More silence from the Skinny-Jeans Kid.

"In other words, we are compelled by international and domestic law to help that country gain and cultivate peaceful nuclear technology."

More silence.

"Which means, we are breaking the law by threatening that country, and we know it."

"But that guy said he wanted to destroy our allies..."

"Ad hominem. Besides, that was a purposeful mis-translation. Try again."

"But it's been proven they are making a weapon..."

"Nope, we've accused them of it with no proof. Our proof of Iraq's WMD was more compelling."

"Whatever pops, go fuck yourself." The Skinny Jeans Kid ceded the bar to Kuraš and walked to an empty booth.

"Ah, a brilliant retort from a stunningly logical mind. Come on, we're just getting started."

Josh/Mike let out a flamboyant *whoop!* but Kuraš was still looking for an adequate adversary. "How can anyone call for death when they haven't even committed recent history to memory. Hell, much less the whole ugly sordid history of this fucked off pseudo-Democracy."

Josh/Mike explained to no one in particular, "Kuraš here knows everything, don't get him going on the History and the Politics."

"I bet that piece of shit doesn't even know why the US still owns a chunk of Cuba."

"It does?" A young woman asked from across Josh/Mike's line of sight.

"Guantanámo Bay. Cuba. Nineteen oh three, Cuban-American Treaty, ring any bells? After the US quote-*liberated*-unquote Cuba from the Spanish they never left. Now we have a fancy torture chamber down there beyond our own legal jurisdiction. Let that paradox sink in."

"I've heard of Guantanámo Bay, but..."

"Well, now 'ya know." Kuraš cut her off.

Another young chap, better suited for fisticuffs than the Skinny-Jeans Kid, asserted from the corner of the bar. "That's bullshit, Cuba was a normal country until Castro showed up and flushed it down the Commie toilet." He had a college sweater on and was acting awfully brave for having wandered too far from his part of the neighborhood.

"From roughly eighteen fourteen to eighteen twenty five the US played pirates of the Caribbean with Spain and the locals. In eighteen twenty two we landed in Cuba, torched a *pirate station*, and remained to *suppress piracy*. In eighteen eighty nine the US declared war on Spain following the Cuban Insurrection and the Cuban War of Independence. What followed was the questionable sinking of the USS Maine in Havana by the Spanish. The US *loves* to sink ships to inspire war. That was the intro to the Spanish-American War, after that we treated Cuba like an abused step-colony until Castro liberated it."

Josh/Mike gushed, "Damn! Did I tell you or what? This guy is like a fucking wiki-page."

"A lot of shit went down before WWI, but you won't likely hear about it unless you look for yourself."

"Like what?" Another young lady asked from beneath a thick black jacket with a demure faux-fur lined collar.

"Like some of the core reasons the Ottoman Empire was involved in WWI as an Axis power go back to the split between the Western and Eastern Roman Empires. Like back when the US was playing around in the Caribbean, we entered into the Second Barbary War." No response from the jacket woman. "That was all the way in Africa, and is also why the Marine Corps' anthem proudly evokes the "Shores of Tripoli." What about Florida being part of Spain, or the President-Monroe-sponsored dispatch of the USS Ontario in eighteen eighteen to assert American claims to Oregon? Unfortunately the Russians and the Spanish felt they still had a claim to Oregon, leading later to the Oregon Treaty of eighteen forty six and the US and Britain telling Russia and Spain to fuck off.

"I can tell by the looks on your faces that a lot was left out of your formal education re: US History. Same here, don't feel special. Most of this information only serves to make you question the innate *awesome* of the good old US-of-A. It's a crime to purposely make our children ignorant, and a crime to act in a way that requires omitting reality out of shame."

"Watch this, guys..." Josh/Mike raised his arms to start the race, "Foreign US military adventures prior to WWI, in chronological order... go!"

"The Quasi-War sort of fits your criteria, eighteen oh one, the First Barbary War, Spanish Mexico, Gulf of Mexico, Spanish West Florida, we have *always* had a hard-on for Florida, Amelia Island, the War of eighteen twelve, Spanish West Florida again, by this time the Spanish are not pleased, Marquesas Islands. Eighteen fifteen–Second Barbary War, Algiers, the *shores of Tripoli*, the First Seminole War, Oregon, we covered Oregon," no one was listening, "Africa, slave-traffic-interception by Act of Congress, Cuba, Puerto Rico. Eighteen twenty seven – Greece, Falkland Islands, Eighteen thirty two – Attack on Quallah Battoo, Sumatra, Indonesia. In eighteen thirty three we started in on Argentina, Peru, Navy Island, Canada, Fiji Islands, eighteen forty one – Taputenea, Gilbert Islands, Samoa, Mexico, China. In eighteen forty three, we return to Africa via the Ivory Coast, then back to Mexico, which helped bring about, the Mexican-American War. Eighteen forty nine – İzmir, Turkey, Ottoman Empire via Jaffa and along the Levant coast. Johanns Island, Argentina, eighteen fifty three – Nicaragua, Japan, Ryūkyū and Bonin Islands, eighteen fifty four – China, then Nicaragua again. Eighteen fifty five – China gets some more, same with Fiji Islands, then Uruguay, and Panama—at the time, a Republic of New Grenada. Then back to China, eighteen fifty seven through fifty eight. Nicaragua, Uruguay, Fiji Islands, once more, then back across the oceans to the Ottoman Empire. On to Paraguay—starting to see why Central and South America aren't so fond of us? Fuck, just wait until the nineteen-eighties. Eighteen fifty nine, Mexico again...really? China, a naval force landed to *protect American interests* in Shanghai. Eighteen sixty – Angola, Portuguese West Africa, Colombia, Japan, Panama, Mexico, China, Nicaragua, Eighteen sixty seven – Formosa – island of Taiwan, Colombia, eighteen seventy – Kingdom of Hawaii, later overthrown completely by the US and occupied permanently. Eighteen eighty two – Egypt, Samoa, Haiti, eighteen ninety one – Bering Strait, where Naval forces sought to stop seal poaching. Was this proto-Greenpeace? Chile, Brazil, and finally, we completely piss the Spanish off and are rewarded with the Spanish-American War. Off to the Philippine Islands, Honduras, nineteen oh three – Syria, nineteen oh three/oh four – Abyssinia, Ethiopia, nineteen oh four – Tangier, Morocco, nineteen twelve – Turkey, nineteen sixteen – China, American forces land to quell a riot taking place on *American property*, whatever that means, in Nanking. Nineteen sixteen – Dominican Republic, nineteen seventeen – China... and finally, World War I."

Kuraš took a long pull from his dark stout.

"Hoooooooo-ly fuck Kuraš." Josh/Mike clapped Kuraš on the back and a few scattered zombies applauded in trickling groups of two before going back to discussing the existential consequences of being *Team Edward* in the same lifetime as being *Team Pacey*.

"You're a genius Kuraš."

"Doesn't matter. Knowing each individual incursion makes no difference if no one sees the insidious *big-picture*." Kuraš murmured.

"Americans are dicks?" Josh/Mike asked sincerely.

"Eh, sort of, but I was driving at the fact that the US has never stopped waging war around the world. By the shape of current events, we appear driven to do so eternally."

"Heavy man."

"You disappoint me Josh/Mike."

"Same here pops."

Kuraš was curious, "How so?"

"Well, if the *big picture* isn't the small picture(s) combined, then you've spent too much time memorizing and not enough time analyzing." Josh/Mike adjusted his faux spectacles and smiled in coy triumph.

"I fucking hate you sometimes."

"You too pops." Josh/Mike leaned in for a patriarchal hug and Kuraš sneered.

An angry voice boomed from a far corner of the bar.

"You have to be out of your mind! How can a living wage be too expensive when our military budget is close to a trillion dollars and we hand out billions in corporate welfare?"

"Hey Kuraš, your boy Socialist Dave might need some back up over there."

"Dave's a big boy Josh/Mike. Stop calling him a Socialist."

07

Someone finally noticed that Jean-Baptisté had a surprisingly articulate mind. Truth be told, this stranger was not blind to Jean-Baptisté's beauty; rather he was puzzled, fascinated, and all-around knocked out that such a mind could be coupled with such a stunning and universally desirable body.

It wasn't fair.

Beneath an amber summer dusk, a bald stranger in a long navy raincoat joined Jean-Baptisté unexpectedly as he drank coffee near his latest photo shoot, in Nowheresville, Okla-Bama.

"May I help you?" Jean-Baptisté asked.

"Indeed."

"I'm not available, so scurry along," Jean-Baptisté waved dismissively. The conversation was beginning to draw the attention of schoolgirls passing the shop on their walk home. The girls stared, stopped still, and began to giggle and vibrate ecstatically. *Ah fuck*, Jean-Baptisté silently lamented. *I've been outed. I haven't even finished my coffee.*

The bald man continued, "The people of the United States need you JB. The people of the Free World need you."

"Get the fuck out of here…"

"I'm being serious JB. Here is my card." *flick*

P. Jonathan Hensley - Central Intelligence Agency - Alexandria, VA.

"I'd like to fly you to Virginia, show you around headquarters, and talk to you about an integral role in securing our national security."

"Isn't that redundant, *securing* security?"

"How about ensuring the security of old Mom and Pops and lovely Lara, no?"

Jean-Baptisté took his card.

"What could I possibly do for the CIA? It's not like I blend into crowds."

"Exactly, quite the opposite. Crowds must bend to you. You automatically have access to rooms and conversations no mere mortal will ever witness. We need you, JB, precisely because they will never see you coming."

Jean-Baptisté was being offered a way to do something meaningful, to be something to someone else—to finally be something in his father's eyes. "What about my work?"

"It is to our advantage that nothing change. Your career will be your cover, of course."

"Of course." Jean-Baptisté felt daft. "There's no number, how do I reach you?"

"I'll get in touch with you JB, you just take some time and think it over. By the by, I'm sure it goes without saying, but discussing this conversation with *anyone* will land you in a detention center instead of a field agency. Understood?" Hensley liked wielding his new position of authority.

"Yes. Mr. Hensley. I mean, Yes, I understand."

08

Keagan walked Sixth Street in a daze. The temperature had dropped and by dusk the waning sunny California skies languished in the sixties. The clouds were low and rain would likely be close behind nightfall. Keagan waited for the cross light instead of jaywalking; bike cops flocked at every intersection.

As he approached the corner of Fifth Street he witnessed a flurry of green mohawk, leather, and chains, pull a man over the railing of the corner dive bar and slam him onto the concrete outside. The mohawked-assailant brought down his clenched fist and knocked the wind out of the stunned man. Downtown Security turned to see what was going on, and the mohawked-man hopped over the fence, "No worries Officer, I'm leavin'."

He bent down into his victim's twisted and mute face. "I find your particular brand of free-market fanaticism disappointing and vile. The people you worship get people like me killed."

The mohawked-man walked away and Keagan tilted his hat. "Where 'ya headed?"

"Somewhere else. What's it to 'ya?"

"My name's Keagan. I find invisible hand economists revolting."

"Well, 'ya better not go in there," The man pointed over his spiked shoulder. "Been taken over by yuppie-spawn and their parasites. My name's Dave. Stupid people call me Socialist Dave. I'm headed home."

"Where 'bouts?"

"Fuck, you writing a book or something?" Socialist Dave growled as he hurried down Spring Street.

"Something like that. I just moved here, and I'm---"

"Sixth and Spring, okay? Are we good?"

"You're the second person I've met from the Lofts. Oh, sorry, from the *building*. I'm down in the basement."

Socialist Dave stopped abruptly. "The basement? There's not supposed to be anyone in the basement."

"It's free; I'm in the Program."

"AA?" Socialist Dave cringed.

"No, nothing like that. I'm in Revision from Nevada."

Socialist Dave eyed him closely, "I thought that was over."

"I probably slipped through." Keagan smiled. He assumed that was impressive, but so far, no one seemed to agree. "Most of the people I met in Nevada had been there a long time."

"They haven't let anyone in or out of the California since the Evictions."

"I'm nothing special, just working on a book set in Los Angeles. I'm sure my publisher glad-handed an official or two." Keagan could feel that he was an unwanted, or at least unexpected presence in the basement.

"Probably doesn't hurt that you're Caucasian and down to wear a suit."

"I doubt my skin tone had anything do with it."

"Are you serious? Why do you think everyone all of a sudden needs Origin papers? Under Revision, your bloodline means as much as your zip code. The whole program is a bigoted sham, an excuse to single out protestors and dissidents. The only people permitted to fast track Revision, are the wealthy and well connected. I'd wager that an Arab last name, or Origin papers from Guatemala would have stopped you cold."

Keagan thought about his hangar-mates in Nevada, he was the only paleface. Every detainee was solidly working class—trapped in the Vegas valley by the construction boom. Marooned without the resources to fight their captivity, and watching their children grow up through digital images. "I see your point."

"When you have an advantage, what matters is how you use it. Come on Mr. Privilege, I'll sell 'ya a drink."

"Sell?"

"I've got me own spot. Welcome to Spring Street, Keagan."

Socialist Dave walked passionately toward their building, through the lobby, and onto an elevator. Keagan followed him down the labyrinthine marble halls of the 11th floor until they reached apartment 1103. Socialist Dave unlocked the apartment; the main room was many times larger than Keagan's entire space, and did not suffer from pathetic, low, painted ceilings. The far wall was composed of immense cantilevered factory windows and brick frames. Keagan approached the open windows and peered down into the immense abyss created by the eleven-story drop to the sub basement common area.

Socialist Dave poured a dark stout from a small homemade tap, "Here, try this."

"Oh, hey," Keagan struggled for something positive to describe the violation his tongue was enduring. "That's, um, strong."

"It's my very own. Slainté. Drinkin' in the neighborhood is more trouble than it's worth, as you witnessed tonight. Since the riots, the fake riots, and the real-fake-riots, you can't cuss down here without a Neighborhood Ambassador coming along and tazing you from his City-bought mountain bike. So I brew my own beer, fuck 'em." Socialist Dave paused for a breath. "Where are you from, Keagan?"

"Vegas, originally."

"No shit."

"You?"

"North Utah. Big family. Nicest people you'll never meet."

"What brought you to LA?"

"Look at me."—Head to toe leather and spikes—"Tiny Orem, Utah couldn't handle the likes of me. Besides, LA is the natural habitat of the

North American mohawked computer animator. It was my destiny. What about you? Why all the effort to leave Sin City?"

"Going back to Nevada was a mistake. Then the laws changed and I got trapped. Making my book take place in Los Angeles seemed like a longshot, but it worked."

"That bad eh?"

"The whole town feeds on addiction. Without the enfeebled and blind, Las Vegas becomes a pothole at the doorstep of Death Valley. Gambling isn't for me; let's just say I'd get more out of piling my money together and lighting it on fire. My parents were drunks, my friends' parents were drunks, our teachers, coaches, and politicians were all playing shepherd to the next generation of enablers. I left the first chance I got and never looked back. Almost never looked back."

"But Revisioning isn't something that just happens. Who's pulling strings for you?"

"Samuel Irvine, the publisher of my first two novels. This is to be the third, the hat trick."

"Pretty sweet deal."

"Too sweet. People like my publisher are strangling the print market. The whole trilogy will be held in a cloud, like a for-pay library."

"No books? I don't trust it. If every method of learning is somehow tied to an internet connection, it's easy to a, censor content, and b, close it off permanently. The power of common people to communicate is subversive. Someone is always trying to find a way to take that back."

"Maybe, but I have my own collection of books."

"What about books that haven't been written yet? What if some asshole two hundred years ago decided to sell out like you are? How many of your favorite authors, important authors, would have been voiceless or drowned out by rubbish?"

"I do see your point Dave. Here's the thing," the stout began to loosen Keagan's tongue, "this isn't my *art*. Between you and I, my books are mediocre at best, predictable at worst."

"Formulaic, contrived..."

"I'm good at plots, good at recycling plots, but no one ever reads my books twice. I harbor a desire to make this one different though. It's going to be my last, I have a feeling."

"*Writer for pay conspires to write magnum opus instead of another trashy best-seller*. Man, even your existential crisis is a cliché."

"Yes, well, I'm no hero. I'm thankful to be thrown this bone."

"You got fucking Stockholm Syndrome, Keagan. Listen to yourself, a sniveling rat apologizing for the complexity of the maze. You're alive and breathing, why isn't that enough? Why must there be something *special* about you?"

"I don't want to suffer."

"I get that, mate, but that's *your* problem, right? What does your self-interest have to do with the rest of us?"

Keagan shrugged. "You ever hear weird shit around here at night?"

"Yeah, sure. Building was mostly empty since when moved in, city noise has always bounced around the hallways."

"Stranger things than that."

"Oh yeah, like what?"

"Loud machinery being dropped, the smell of crushed cigarettes, muffled voices, some CRASS once..."

"Well, this place went from being a bank after the Depression, to being a deadly sweatshop. Scores of people died working here. No one really knows what's in half of these rooms."

"That's not very helpful. I'm not superstitious, so I'm left feeling a little like my mind is having some fun with me."

"Echoes down there are a bitch, lad. Don't go getting yer'self worked up over nothin'."

Socialist Dave had a point.

"You said something about people getting *evicted* earlier, and I pretended to know what you meant."

Socialist Dave shook his head. "You really have been under a rock."

"On a cot, in a drone hanger."

"You're familiar with the Occupation at Zuccotti Park, correct?"

"Maybe?"

"NYPD kettles, beats, and pepper sprays, peaceful protestors, which leads to thousands of people occupying Wall Street?"

"Yes, okay. Not pretending this time, yes I remember."

"In a few months, Occupations all over the US took over public spaces and mounted massive marches."

"Was there one here?"

"Right down Spring Street, encircling City Hall. It was glorious."

"What happened?"

"They were Evicted. New York was first, but city by city SWAT teams in body armor with AR-15s and tear gas arrested, and tortured tens of thousands of Americans."

"But no one died, right?"

"What difference does that make? As long as no one dies, the First Amendment can be trampled on?"

"No, just that it could have been worse."

"Maybe. I lost a dear friend during the LA Eviction."

"I'm sorry Dave, I'm an idiot."

"Orin went alone on the night of the Eviction, to face the LAPD and resist. He got caught up in a group of protestors that spontaneously began to fight back against the black uniforms. He was struck in the knees by batons and collapsed. He died with an LAPD boot on his neck."

"Fuck."

"It get's fuckin' worse. His wife spent the next year caught up in courts fighting for her freedom. After the Evictions, the Occupations were deemed a domestic terrorist threat and everyone, myself included, got rounded up and bio-scanned. When she sued for Orin's wrongful death, the conversation always turned to her husband's involvement in subversive activities. They let the young rookie that killed him go. The cop was green, and seemed genuinely shocked and horrified that Orin had died. He was no good as a stormtrooper after that."

"How was this not on the news?"

"Some of it was, you know how it works. Your precious Revision program was the first Federal strike. Some Nazi in Ohio floated the idea of preventing large demonstrations by inhibiting interstate travel. It started as border-style checkpoints but the potential for quelling *all* mass gatherings proved too attractive and now," Dave concluded in a poorly executed German accent, "we must all *show ze papers*."

"Maybe I moved here at the wrong time."

"It's the whole country man. Stand your ground, Keagan. We are. Speaking of which, my remaining roommate is due home soon, and I'm as drunk as I'd like to get tonight, so…"

"Does that mean goodbye?" Keagan finished his pint.

"No, that means, piss the fuck off."

Keagan waited patiently before three steel elevator doors. The far left car stopped, but the doors remained shut. Fingers pressed through the gap between the metal doors, then hands, wrists, arms, and finally Dodger Blue eyes fixed in determined anger on the wall across the landing. Keagan moved to help but was too late, Cadence pressed through the stubborn doors and kicked both as they slowly slid closed and the elevator car fled.

"Fuck you." Cadence snarled at the retreating lift.

"Pretty obnoxious, eh?" Keagan interjected.

"Oh, look, it's basement boy."

"I just met another building mate. Nice chap."

"Bully for you." She curtsied, fumbling to pick up several small, shoebox-sized containers. "Ta for now."

And off she went into 1103.

The elevator arrived. Keagan stepped in, suppressing a wide smile, and pressed "B." Perhaps this meant he'd see her again soon.

FRIDAY

09

When Lara rushed into the restaurant from a windy and rain-sodden night, the staff and patrons paused, memorializing their brief, unrestricted sight. Similarly, dinner and service were interrupted as Jean-Baptisté ripped his raincoat off, lustfully...or so it seemed to his swooning admirers. The maître d fumbled with his podium and reservation book. "My sincere apologies, right this way."

It had been years since Lara's hair had seen black dye or industrial grade hairspray and rolling pins. Though her clothing still reflected her worship of utility, she no longer trolled estate sales for alterable antiques. Jean-Baptisté still dressed like a young Marlon Brando, but no longer greased his wavy hair to his head. He, as his agent put it, *thankfully* no longer required constant vigil against tattoos.

Lara had already succumbed to a large, incomplete back piece of a wonderful hanging garden whose tangled flora wrapped her arms in color. It was a safe place to escape when the world became too hateful. The reaching, conical design terminated at a single flower above a phone number, crudely tattooed on her wrist. The tattoo meant Jean-Baptisté belonged to her.

The couple were seated immediately and ordered.

"Look at you my handsome man." Lara flirted over their clasped hands, bridging the small white-clothed table, alight with silver and porcelain saucers.

"I'd rather look at you, the view from my side is astonishing..." Jean-Baptisté pressed his lips to her fingers and looked into her eyes.

"Take me away sir."

"Where my love?"

"Anywhere."

"I may be doing just that, very soon."

Their drinks arrived. They toasted to one another and to the unjust state of bliss they lived in.

"So...taking you away..." Jean-Baptisté set his glass on the fine tablecloth. "I have a new account."

"Anyone I know?"

"It will be international, it will mean a steep up-front fee for yours truly, and it's not an exclusive; I can keep doing my print work. It's win-win." Jean-Baptisté took another sip from his neat scotch.

He's trying to sell me something... Lara thought as Jean-Baptisté drained his pint glass and smiled at her. "It sounds like an incredible deal, my love. What's the catch?"

"I don't know yet. All I know is that I can't tell you how incredibly high up the food chain my future employer is, and how much I'll have, like, a life-fulfilling experience where my work actually *helps* people," Jean-Baptisté stopped, he had gone too far.

"Oh, is it a 501(c)?"

"I can't say. But look, my love, it sounds too good to be true, I know this, but I *have* to go."

Lara smiled, "Of course. I would never stand in your way. Never."

"Ah, you are too perfect, I am a very lucky man."

That smug fucking smile. "And I, a lucky lady."

They kissed...and again...as dinner arrived.

"I have to leave in the morning and fly to Alexandria for a few days."

"Egypt?" Lara asked, genuinely confused and excited.

"No, pretty lady. Virginia. The rep is in Alexandria, I have to do a three-d sell. Some exec requested a one-on-one before we start signing contracts."

Weird, Lara thought. "You said you already had the job."

"I do, I mean, it's a slam dunk."

"So tell me, why all the suspense?"

"I can't." Jean-Baptisté could not hide his conflict. He was dangerously close to lying to his beloved.

"Sure, but I'm your wife," Lara flirted. "I can't even testify against you."

"Lara, please." Jean-Baptisté had never before raised his voice in her presence. "I cannot speak of it, not yet. Let's drop the subject."

"Of course." Lara trembled. Images of Jean-Baptisté's adoring fans, begging on their knees before him, flooded her mind. She knew she had to hurt him for making her feel that way, for making her doubt. She needed to fill his mind with a plague of indelible thoughts.

The gleaming couple ate in bitter silence and had to request that the restaurant insulate them from patrons coming by to express astonishment at having run across the couple in public. They were happy; they tried to remember.

Morning came and Jean-Baptisté rose to dress and prepare for his flight. After a warm shower and hot coffee he returned to the bedroom. Lara lay silently on the bed. He didn't know how to ease her mind without risking his new opportunity. *She will understand soon.*

Lara listened to Jean-Baptisté's movements, her eyes remained closed and she spoke not a word. Jean-Baptisté kissed her lightly on the forehead and locked the door behind him.

Lara's emerald eyes opened and she slowly rose from the bed.

LAX was bursting at the seams but Lara caught a glimpse of Jean-Baptisté at the security gate. A young TSA officer's eyes widened and she clasped her hands over her mouth. "It's him, look girl, it's Jean-Baptisté, holy shit."

Jean-Baptisté only smiled. The young woman touched her husband a bit too often for Lara's taste, but her husband didn't seem to mind.

A heavy hand came to rest on Lara's shoulder. "Excuse me. I couldn't help but notice that you are an incredibly stunning woman."

"Go away." Lara shrugged off the interruption. Jean-Baptisté was being hugged by every female TSA officer at the gate, one pretended she had to frisk him.

"Come on. Let me buy you a drink. You look like you need one. I'm the kind of guy to give it to you, I mean, buy you one."

Lara saw his lips moving but heard no sound. The man was only a faint cloud of cheap tequila with tiny angry eyes. Lara punched him in the throat and he collapsed to the ground. Shallow, terrified breaths pushed between his panicked lips.

Lara bent down and looked at the man. Like a widow inspecting a form caught in its web, she hovered, waiting with pleasure as he choked.

Jean-Baptisté was gone.

A gush of sincere tears from her delicate, piercing eyes created unwanted attention throughout the bustling international-airport and parking garage.

Lara sat calmly in her car, staring forward, composing herself. She dried those tears, taking care to wait until the last of them had marred her cheekbones and soiled her facade. A smile spread across her lips and for a moment she felt her wrath wane. Jean-Baptisté did not hold the ends of her universe in his beautiful, monstrous hands. For a brief moment, she felt free.

Lara removed a blade from her small leather sheath and placed it quietly on her lap. She clutched the hem of her dress and pulled the pliant material, slowly, until her thighs rested, trembling and exposed, beneath the filthy fluorescent daylight. As she scolded herself for doubting *their* love, doubting *his* strength, doubting *her* faith, she interrupted the intimate white flesh of her thighs with red, bellicose streaks of lightning. As she had for years—more than she dared to recall.

Perfection is only temporal; perfection is as circumstantial as imperfection. Lara was dedicated mind and body to the illusion of perfection—to impressing *Them*. Jean-Baptisté, beautiful, honorable, and decent as he was, could not keep her from lusting after his unchallenged attention. Pain gave her control, but knowing that perfection brought her insufferable woe had always been argument enough. Jean-Baptisté would never understand; had she straddled him and run herself through with a martyr's blade, he would have asked *Why so violent?*

To *him*, they were perfect, to *him* nothing else made sense, to *him* the conversation need not be had. Either Jean-Baptisté was a higher quality of human than Lara, or he was lying through his perfect teeth.

10

Kuraš came to Los Angeles with his family in the roaring Nineteen-Eighties; his final years of public education. He wandered its cramped byways feeling trapped, hemmed in, but unprepared to react. After high school he attempted to live in the vast expanses of the Midwest and the South, but like many who spend their formative years in the City, Kuraš felt himself lulled back, kicking and screaming.

Kuraš took a sensible job with the City—a career, he hoped. After the financial collapse, he took a pay cut and stayed on, repairing the City's forgotten infrastructure. Kuraš was nowhere near retirement when the Mayor decided to clean house as a show of fiscal accountability. Thirty-four hundred City employees were quietly asked to accept a lump-sum disability estimate rather than waiting for their pension upon retirement. Employees would have no concerns for their health, (so long as the City remained in existence) and as a bonus, slick, young consultants would guide them through the process of *re-investing for their future.*

Kuraš had wondered aloud during the department meeting, "The people who tanked our entire economy want to handle my retirement? Are you all insane?"

He was escorted from the meeting. "Fuck those guys," Kuraš reasoned, "I'm cashing out." He refused to leave it in a bank, credit union, or brokerage, so he liquidated his after-taxes payout, and stashed it in secure places all over Los Angeles County. Kuraš' Spartan lifestyle allowed him to make meager withdrawals, for food, cigarettes, books, and gasoline.

Kuraš smoked a cigarette on the northeast corner of Kohler Street and Seventh; when he felt comfortable that no one had followed him through Skid Row he walked rapidly to a locked box in the bowels of the Seventh Street Post Office. Kuraš had been held up five times using this stash-spot, twice at knifepoint and three by pistol. He had talked all five assailants into joining him for a pitcher of beer instead of risking being rolled up for aggravated assault. This made Kuraš something of a celebrity at the Skid Row saloons.

Kuraš cleared out his PO box and locked it.

The ground floor of the Alexandria Hotel was distended, groaning at the seams. The joyous chaos of a chalk graffiti protest flooded both sides of the corner bar's slim iron divider. Socialist Dave was ranting at the bar, Cadence was nowhere in sight, and Kuraš had no stomach for Josh/ Mike. He waded upstream through the bachanalists, and envisioned clearing a path with a sturdy fuel-dripping blowtorch; he smiled quietly and walked against the flashing red hand.

Spring Street was shut down during all confrontation, the result of accumulated downtown business organizations (DBOs) that sprung from the fertile ashes of city government like a flagrant sea of fungus. These DBOs aped the status quo, enforcing their policies via private Neighborhood Ambassadors, heavily armed and beyond traditional jurisdictional reach. Shutting down streets to keep the New Downtowners happy in their various distractions—bicycle lanes, cooperative farmer's markets—made more sense to private business than it had to the City. The corporation—like the Catholic Church before them—understood that minor cultural concessions would make or break the master-servant dichotomy.

Kuraš whistled as he walked south on Spring Street and pulled a small knife from his jacket. He dipped casually near the right front tires of six parked police cars and, without missing a step, stabbed each in turn.

He resented that these protests lacked any sacrifice. They were Kabuki Theater that turned his building's front step into an arcane flesh-pressing orgy of misplaced fashion sense and a trite drunken waterfall of conversations.

Safely upstairs, Kuraš poured a drink and sat next to his open bay of windows. His idea of furnishing a room involved locating a place for his ass, a place for his feet near the place for his ass, and preferably a place near both to place an ashtray, and/or a source of light. Kuraš dropped his feet on a dining table chair (though he had never secured a dining table to match) and balanced a white ashtray on his soft black work pants.

As the Pacific strangled the earnest summer sun, the impenetrable walls of commerce and finance were replaced by the glow of implied security against frigid, antagonistic streets. Kuraš listened to the people below, playing music, beating drums, yelling, and asking for approval.

SATURDAY

11

The sunrise began to rain down on Kuraš' apartment. As time progressed, the light warmed an angular and growing chasm between improbable heat and the still sleeping.

After a short frenzy of rote activities Kuraš climbed to the pool deck on the roof of the building with his coffee, his cigarettes, and the last of his pre-rolled---

"Kuraš. It's good to see you." A thick man at the top of the stairs extended his hand to Kuraš, who took the final three steps slowly and left the man's hand empty.

"Do you recognize me, Kuraš?"

"Of course. Why are you here? I am doing just fine, you know."

"I'm not here to scrutinize you Kuraš, quite the opposite. I'm here to ask for your help."

"Help? From me? Bullshit."

Kuraš had not seen the man since his state-monitored rehabilitation at Lompoc. He certainly had not expected to see him here, now. Kuraš was ordered to serve at minimum-security FCI Lompoc, but was sent—by administrative error—to maximum security USP Lompoc.

"Do you remember your cell mate?"

"Maybe, why?"

The thick man waked toward the long outdoor sofas at the edge of the pool deck and seated himself. "He's out, he's been out for about five years. Got caught up in some protests, and he's on the run now. I think he's a good kid but my hands are tied. With the Insurrection Protection Act sliding through Congress he has a limited amount of time."

"Never heard of it."

"No one has, it is a part of a closed-door committee on the economy. We are doing our best to keep people out of prison, but any record of civil disobedience, especially in connection with the Occupations, has become sufficient evidence for detention."

"It's your *job* to lock people up."

"Bad guys Kuraš. I lock up bad guys. Your cellmate has been in and out of custody since nineteen ninety one."

"Ninety-nine. He went down with the World Trade Organization protests. He never stopped talking about it." Kuraš searched for his joint.

The thick man smiled tiredly.

"He was arrested in ninety one and became an FBI asset. They made him part of a sting operation in Seattle."

"Agent Provocateur?"

"Something like that. His staged arrest laid the groundwork for later legal arguments in favor of indefinite detention. He managed to get away this time."

"This time?"

"When LAPD stormed City Hall, the clash escalated, and he slipped into the masses and disappeared."

"How?"

"We don't know. But he called me when he surfaced."

"That's some pretty important information."

"Look Kuraš, we've been running him around town looking for an out. The rest of the City is overrun with private battalions, the more the merrier on the west side. It's becoming impossible to-"

"So, what the hell do you want with me?"

"I trust you."

Kuraš huffed, "Good luck with that. Give my daughter Shannon a call and ask her if it's a good idea to."

"I know where your conscience falls on important matters. I need to pull him out of Los Angeles, under the City's radar."

"So you need a safehouse."

"I do."

"I live in a loft, my life is about as private as a fishbowl on a five-story pole."

"Walk with me Kuraš," the thick man escorted him to the staircase leading from the roof onto the thirteenth floor, "are you familiar with the Revision Program?"

"What about it?"

"Revisioning has been indefinitely postponed until the Occupation movements are sufficiently depleted. Your basement was retrofitted for security and is now abandoned. We think that makes your basement perfect."

"That's what makes me nervous. What would stop the rest of the pigs from thinking it's perfect?"

"We just need you to keep an eye, an ear, and whatever else you have to spare, on the basement floor. Can you do that?" The man asked sincerely.

"I can." The whole thing felt like a setup, but the thick man represented the only time prison had breathed down Kuraš' neck. Saying no would bring the full weight of the LAPD down on the building. If he refused, they'd be under surveillance at the very least. "When is this happening?"

"Right away."

"Send him down to the corner pub on Tuesday. I'll scoop him up and make arrangements."

"The people of the United States thank you Kuraš." The thick man smiled and tried the handshake again.

"The people of the United States can kiss my ancient ass."

12

Will & Liam had been waiting. The stylish new restaurant they chose on Main Street was given "" according to Liam. By whom, he would not divulge.

"That would be vulgar."

The staff put their first drinks in front of them, took their order, and melted into the walls—invisible.

Will looked around for their waiter, for *any* waiter. "For fuck's sake, people."

"Relax Will." Liam motioned to the Host. "Ma'am?"

The young girl approached shyly, her cheeks were twin rosebuds of unexpected flattery. "I'm no ma'am sir, I'm only..."

"My parents are both southern my darling, please pardon my manners."

"Oh no, I didn't mean to..."

"Quite all right. The gentleman and I were wondering if something had gone wrong with our order."

Will had no patience for the game, "And another round of drinks. Soon. Please."

"Don't mind him m'lovely. We will take two more drinks, at your leisure. Thank you kindly."

The host slipped away on hospital grade sneakers with her hands clasped ecstatically behind her back.

"You're disgusting. She's like, fifteen."

"I beg your pardon."

"Beg all you like."

"I treated her with the respect I would afford an adult, she took it as flirtation, so be it. Being gruff and unsatisfied will not make our service better my friend, quite the opposite."

"Whatever. We need to discuss what goes down with the ex-mas revolt. I'm working on the triage pictures from the first front and I need to know how, well, *what*, I'm transitioning into."

"I'm not certain I am in love with making this into a *war*." Liam carefully folded his napkin until it resembled the dark brown kerchief in his suit pocket.

"It was your fucking idea." Will untucked part of his t-shirt that had accidentally pushed into his baggy canvas shorts.

"I know, I know." Liam placed his chin on his folded hands. "I keep seeing images of injury, the end justifying the means, i.e. the casualties of war = the death of ex-mas, but that's precisely what the church and our government do: candy-coat, apologize for, and explain away atrocity."

"You have got to be kidding me. We're never going to finish this fucking thing..."

"Stick with me," Liam wrapped his arm around Will's shoulder, "the information is an *awakening,* and there is a *general strike* by the children to hold the adults accountable for lying to them, for deceiving their very own children for centuries."

"Okay, okay, I like that, a slow awakening?"

"Yes, intellectual, and underground."

"Terrorist cells of enlightened toddlers..."

"No, no, no, more like French Resistance to Nazi occupation."

"What?"

"No, that's no good either. Shit." Liam sat back and ran his fingers along the rim of his empty glass.

"Go back to the strike idea." Will prodded.

"General Strike, no more chores, *no chores without representation?*"

"Yes," Will laughed.

"Committees to collect parental confessions, blacklists..."

"No play dates with the following families: McNeel, Miller, Sucgang, Spell..."

"...until we are treated as..."

"...equals..."

"...well, equals may be pushing it."

"Yet Politburo-style *Committees* wasn't pushing it?"

"Tamer by comparison," Liam was serious.

"Let's start again," Will sighed. "Where in the fuck is our food?"

13

The sun shined brightly into the massive chasm formed by the interior walls of the Spring Street building. Ribbons of soft white light filtered through noxious clouds and rained down life giving missives. Lara pushed her loft's large levered window open and greeted her small garden with delight. Each budding conical flower whispered a soft serenade, which bounced from one hemisphere of her mind to the next —a ballet of chlorophyll, and pricking, angled leaves that coddled the flower's precious spiked seed. Lara moved her delicate fingertips along the sun-drenched leaves and touched the engorged, thorny seed waiting beneath petals of swirled white and violet. "Soon, my loves. Soon."

Lara touched each plant with care, giving her body's heat to the small creatures. They had been with her for many years now. Her tiny garden began as a dark concern, long before Jean-Baptisté. She was owned back then, and in her subservience, her rhythmic freedom sputtered. Lara could never completely submit, and so she kept her deadly garden as insurance against darker days. The garden flourished and Lara bore her abysmal pride silently. The flowers graced the windowsill with strained, purple-muddled light and angular, cast-green shadows. After the sun's light waned, Lara's beauties curled in defense around their precious, spined seed, precursor to an act of attrition.

§

Lara's family had known difficult times in America. The Connors had arrived in Texas in 1832. The Connor boys signed on to defend Coahuila y Tejás from the Mexican government and bled Éire's green during the Battle of San Jacinto. Five of the six brothers lost their lives, but Pleasant D. Connor survived, ironically, by being the first man wounded in the seminal battle. He listened to the chaos of war from a cot and received his brothers' Commanding Officers as they arrived, one by one, to announce the Connor Boys' untimely demise.

Pleasant D. Connor gathered his wounds, misery, and the remaining Connor women to cross the border into the Louisiana badlands near the outlet of Sabine Lake. He fenced thirty forgotten acres of dense, brutal bayou and built a simple home for the family. Sarah, Rachel, Beatrice, Hazel, Shirley, and Barbara Connor transformed the angry, resistant land into workable gardens and a grazing plain for livestock.

On a day, not too warm, and not too wet, Pleasant loaded as many of the Connors as he could onto his horse-drawn wagon and began the slow trip into Johnson's Bayou. The others walked alongside the wagon, taking turns with its occupants. The trip was the first contact the Connor women had experienced with the outside world since leaving Texas. Pleasant D. had been able to find work in Johnson's Bayou, re-fitting steel-band wheels, and constructing farm equipment for the local agricultural bulkheads. The townspeople called him "Mac," and when he entered the town limits with six women and twenty-seven children, the townspeople took wary notice.

The Connor family spent a magical day walking in and out of shops selling fine dresses all the way from New York and silks pilfered from ships docked in New Orleans. The bustling metropolitan complex of shops, banks, and dining rooms mesmerized Rachel's only daughter Catherine. Her youthful curiosity led her away from the family and soon she was outside of both eye line and earshot.

The sun began to set through the drooping willows as Pleasant D. collected the Connor family to head back into the inky Bayou. Catherine was nowhere to be found. The family fanned out into the three streets composing Johnson's Bayou. Rachel spotted Catherine sitting on a hitching post next to a handsome man.

"I apologize if she has inconvenienced you sir." Rachel grabbed Catherine's hand and pulled her from the post.

"Not at all Madame, she is a joy and truly, an astonishingly beautiful child. I can see, she must make her lovely mother very proud." The strange man had a stern and angular face, mysteriously amber eyes, and a long lithe body that seemed alien to Rachel; her understanding of men was that they were short, hairy, and pugilistic versions of women. When the man tried to kiss Rachel's hand she flushed crimson and could not look him in the eye.

"What is your name, Madame?"

Rachel pulled her hand away, "I am a widow," she corrected him. "Thank you kindly for being polite to the child."

"My apologies Madame...Mademoiselle." the strange man removed his hat and bowed to Rachel and Catherine. "Please permit me to take you and your daughter for a humble meal at my home."

"No, we really could not accept..."

"I insist." The strange man stood firm.

"You may insist all you like, it is not possible." Rachel escorted Catherine away, and hid her vibrant smile from the strange man.

"I will try again and again until you accept..."

Rachel stopped and turned slowly, "If you must, speak to Pleasant D. Connor, and he will discuss the matter with you."

"The repairman?" The handsome stranger asked.

"Yes, he is the wheel repairman and my brother."

"He attends you?"

"Yes." Rachel gathered her skirts and walked proudly back to the city center to re-group with her tribe. Rachel sat in the back of the wagon with Catherine on her lap. A secret and perfect thought wandered through her young mind—she may be rescued.

"Rachel! Where is Rachel?" Pleasant D. looked around the humble dining room as the Connor sisters set the table and finished preparing dinner. They all shrugged in ignorance. Pleasant roared, "Find her. Now."

Beatrice found Rachel and Catherine sitting beneath a large weeping willow on the edge of the property. "Get back to the house child, Pop is upset."

"Why is he upset?"

"I can't say, he blew in from Johnson's Bayou full of piss and vinegar and wanting to see you. Specifically."

Rachel's smile faded. "This can't be good..."

As the women began to take their places at the table, Beatrice entered with Rachel and Catherine. The silent gathering stared at the accused during the long walk to the gallows. Pleasant D. entered and took his place at the head of the table. As dinner came to a slow end and the Connor sisters began clearing dishes from the table, Pleasant D. asked Rachel to remain.

"Rachel, you are my youngest brother's bride, may he rest in peace, and as such I have always feared that the day would come to make a very important decision. Among your sisters, you show the greatest promise for capturing a husband, and I'll admit it to your face, that you are indeed the loveliest of the Connor sisters, my dear and sainted Sarah, excepted of course."

"Of course," Rachel nodded.

"I want no part in defiling my dear brother's memory, but I cannot stand in the face of Nature and deny that you may still make a fine wife some day. No self-respecting man would take a used-up woman as his bride, but he may still desire a source of pride, a source of arrogance, and you can still provide such a thing. Do you understand?"

"I think so, why are you telling me this?"

"Thaddeus Monroe came into the shop today."

Rachel blushed violet and turned her head.

"Yes, I can see you know of whom I speak."

"I do, but I did not know his name. I admonished him for being so forward."

"He did not accept that as a proper answer, and today he came to ask for your hand in courtship."

Rachel remained silent; dancing-laughter and joy rang in her skull like the bells of Notre Dame.

"I am considering this offer. Mr. Monroe is a surveyor for the government, he was sent here to map and survey lots for some law called the 'Homestead Act.' He's here all the way from Baltimore."

"Is that far?"

"It may as well be the old country, Rachel." Pleasant D. looked her in the eye, "This may be very important for the family." Rachel was the youngest wife, she and her husband had only been blessed with one child before his untimely death, and though she tried, Rachel showed none of the necessary tenacity to push a plow or conduct anything above and beyond standard domestic hygiene.

"This man would like to help us, Rachel. Our home is in danger of being stolen by the government. He feels confident that he can place our land into what he calls a 'grandfather clause' and save the farm at least."

"I see."

"I will tend to all arrangements."

"What about-"

"That is my final word." Pleasant D. dismissed Rachel.

Thaddeus began sending quaint hand-written missives for Rachel and gifts for Catherine. Each day as Pleasant D. arrived home from work; she waited to see if the strange man had sent another desperate description of his agonized life without her. She fell deeply into love with this man's charisma, certainty, and indelible drive. *All this for me?* she'd think, swollen with pride and hope.

When the courtship had come to an end, Pleasant D. loaded Rachel, Catherine, and their meager belongings into his wagon and they set off before sunrise for Johnson's Bayou. Thaddeus purchased a small home on the corner of a successful plantation, and by the time the Connors arrived workers had prepared the home for his bride and daughter. The formality and ceremony of exchanging Rachel's hand for a dowry had the three-times-removed feeling of an ancient tale of kingdoms seeking peace through betrothed progeny. Pleasant D. shook Thaddeus' hand and walked out the front door.

"My love," Thaddeus gushed as he approached Rachel, "come here."

Rachel obeyed and they embraced. Her fears that Thaddeus would morph into a cruel and despotic man the moment Pleasant D. left had been allayed.

Rachel's days and nights took a delicious and sensual turn. Fine foods, silks, and the creamiest of European chocolates were at all times, at her fingertips, courtesy of her gushing and prideful husband.

Upon her thirteenth birthday, Thaddeus insisted that Catherine join him during his workday several times per week. Rachel was ecstatic for her young daughter to be given the gift of *male-entrusted* knowledge. She passionately de-briefed Catherine after every visit until Catherine stopped responding. Rachel stopped asking and Catherine dutifully took her place next to Thaddeus each week as he rode deep into the unmapped bayous of south Louisiana.

Catherine fell ill and Rachel kept her close to her at all times. Her body became swollen and each day she was burdened with a nausea that frightened her young mind. Rachel cried silently in the kitchen as Catherine watched her from the dining table.

"Mother?"

Rachel stood, hunched at the shoulders, keeping herself upright with the strength of the counter.

"Who was it Catherine?"

"I don't know what you-"

"Do not lie to me child!" Rachel spun and took Catherine's delicate jaw into her hand. "I knew this day would come, it was only a matter of time."

"Mother, I…"

"Tell me child, or on my mother's grave I will throttle you and this bastard child senseless."

"I don't know who it was."

"You lay with a man, and you don't even know who he is?"

"No. I mean..."

"Ah, then there are many; my daughter is a whore." Rachel began crying again and seated herself, defeated, next to her sobbing daughter. "I cannot bear this Catherine, I cannot..."

"It was Thaddeus."

Rachel rose from her stupor. "How dare you,"

"I'm sorry mother, I'm sorry---"

Rachel pulled her daughter into her arms, "It doesn't matter who it was. We will get through this. I will never leave your side. Do you understand?"

"Yes momma, I understand." Catherine's youthful countenance and Rachel's ruptured heart were streaked with tears.

Rachel and Catherine united in preparation. The tragedy and pain of a fatherless child was superseded by the joy of a newborn. Each detail was finely accounted for with love. Yet Rachel could not forget her daughter's accusation, and could not rest soundly that the child was lying.

"Thaddeus?"

"Yes?" Thaddeus looked up from his scattered collection of maps, instrumentation, and dull pencils.

"Have you heard anything about the child's father? Anything at all?"

"I have not," he answered curtly.

Rachel waited a moment until Thaddeus disengaged from his calculations, "Have you tried my love? It is indeed a small town, surely someone has heard..."

Thaddeus stared pitifully at Rachel. "You are a very simple woman. No one will be bragging about that in town, believe me. The child is stunning, no one will remark otherwise. To deflower such a creature would swell any man with pride. It would soil that pride to admit a bastard seed. Let's speak of it no more."

"*You did this.*" Rachel whispered.

"Did you speak?" Thaddeus roared.

"I did not," Rachel responded quietly. "Good night, please rest well, I will see you in the morning."

"Goodnight Rachel, give us a kiss before bed? That's a good girl, thank you."

On first opportunity, Rachel spirited Catherine away from the plantation. She burst, half-dressed (for the time) into the wheel repair shop on Lexington Ave.

"My god, Rachel!" Pleasant D. rose from his chair near an anvil.

Rachel placed her hand over his mouth, begging him to be silent. "Come with me." Rachel pulled Pleasant D. and Catherine into the shop's small stockroom and drew the curtain behind them.

"The child is pregnant."

"Catherine?" Pleasant D. turned and knelt next to Catherine, "Darling is this true?" He unconsciously ran his hand over her swollen belly. "What have you let happen woman?" Pleasant D. cursed Rachel with his hand raised.

"It was your business partner, her patron," Rachel answered confidently, daring him to strike her.

Pleasant D. dropped his eyes, lost in thought. "We must leave. Now."

"What do you mean? He deserves death for harming this child."

"He is a very powerful man Rachel. We'll all be dead by Sunday if he's hurt."

Pleasant D. locked the shop and they rode as fast as his rickety wagon would take them, back to the recesses of the south Louisiana bayou. Pleasant D. was silent for the entire trip and only spoke softly into Sarah's ear when they arrived. Sarah's eyes widened and she looked down at Catherine over Pleasant D.'s shoulder. When he had finished speaking he walked into their bedroom and locked the door.

"Children, sisters, please come together, we have much work to do and very little time to do it."

The Connors had inherited a long tradition of expulsion and defeat; with these lessons came the gifts of courage and honorable death. Acting on the instruction of the Connor women before her, Sarah delegated duties to the sisters and children.

"Go, now, and do not dally. "

Thaddeus took his complaint to the local constable. With the lawman in rapt attention, Thaddeus wove an immaculate tapestry of a heathen polygamist compound in the deep bayou, a coven of pagan witches and their demon offspring, headed by a thieving sex-crazed Scotsman. Thaddeus' station as an agent of the government convinced Governor Hébert to dispatch a rather large sliver of the State's Militia to Johnson's Bayou.

Militia troops were led, at Thaddeus' behest, to the Connor land. The commander was himself a Scot and felt it prudent to take all precautions. The family had no doubt set up a defensive perimeter.

"Scot? Did I say Scot? No, he's a thieving Irishman."

The commander mounted his horse. "Irish? That's a bit worse now isn't it Mr. Monroe?"

"Are you insane man? He's a simple wheel fitter!" Thaddeus screamed as the consuming bayou heat peeled away both his patience and decorum.

"I do not expect you to understand. You are not the kind of man who has had to face the violent unknown."

When they reached the perimeter fence the soldiers found no improvised projectiles or explosives. The commander knelt down next to a fence pole. He quietly looked at the aged, cracking wood, "They are waiting for us."

"What do you mean sir?" An eager private studied the fence to no avail.

"The red and blue streaks on the posts. I'd wager that every post in the entire perimeter has been conspicuously streaked."

"What does it mean?"

"It means they saved us some trouble by not enforcing the perimeter. It is a minor offer of peace, a stalemate."

"Turn around and go home."

"...or die."

"But they couldn't possibly overpower us." The soldier added; defiance that he and other soldiers often mistook for courage.

The commander ordered his troops to set up camp at the fenceline and to organize patrols to ensure that the family did not steal away in the dark of night. All slept uneasily. Thaddeus greeted the dawn, still smoking short cigars and pacing. By the end of the day the child would be his.

"Commander!" A private rushed into the commander's tent.

"You had better-"

"Sir!" The private saluted.

"At ease soldier."

"This landed in the center of camp this morning." The private produced a long arrow-like projectile. The weapon was tipped in tempered metal. "It reads, 'We will approach your camp by half-noon, we come in peace, we come to understand why you are here, and to offer our assistance.' What should we do sir?"

"We'll have visitors soon. Set up a camp perimeter beyond the foliage and gather my men in parade formation before my tent."

The commander watched as three women and one child approached from across a soft emerald meadow. The women stopped several hundred yards before reaching the fenceline.

"Let's go," the commander stepped forward and his handpicked, ten-soldier detail pulled away from the gathered platoon.

The detail led the commander into the meadow and created an armed human shield, with weapons pointed in all directions but aft. The young women were seated when the detail reached them. They had arranged a small table, tea setting, and two chairs.

"Please join us sir." Beatrice offered.

The commander approached the women and took a seat across from small, stained circles of inherited china. He looked at the women carefully. All three were spun of fine silk, each a sullen and untarnished beauty. It seemed that Connor was indeed keeping to himself for good reason. "Which of you is Rachel?"

"I am sir," Rachel moved forward and pushed Catherine behind her.

"Is that the child?"

"Yes. Sir."

"All Mr. Monroe desires is your return. If you must stay amongst your people, then I am to bring the child to his home this evening."

"Neither is possible sir, I'm sure Mr. Monroe can explain perfectly why we are no longer obligated by his command."

"Yes, he told us everything. Your witches' coven is not welcome in this community Mrs. Monroe. I need not point out that the Louisiana Government is composed of god-fearing Christian men."

"But we are not..."

Barbara placed the finest cup and saucer in the commander's hand. "Please sir, it is our own, brought from Cork."

His Gaelic blood could not resist, "Thank you. I regret that this is our introduction." The commander held his cup high and sipped strongly of the fragrant and dark tea. "My, that is exceptional."

Beatrice began to flirt. Pleasant D. had asked them all to, but Rachel and Catherine found the mere thought impossibly repellant.

"Tell me your names."

"I am Barbara," the fifth eldest sister confessed shyly.

"I am Beatrice," the eldest Connor sister whispered coyly into the commander's ear.

"Yes. This is all quite a pity Rachel, wouldn't you say? Shouldn't we all just go up to the house and talk this out civilly?"

71

"Do you see how your men are looking at my child?" Rachel asked calmly.

The commander was not blind. In spite of Beatrice's charm and Barbara's devastating youth, the men were leering provocatively at Catherine. Though her abdomen rose, heavy and distended with child, she cast a spell that permeated his subordinates' libidos.

He did not answer Rachel and she could hold her tongue no longer. "Your dear Mr. Monroe is responsible for this, responsible because it is his seed, forced upon a child in his care."

"Mr. Monroe is not here to answer such a charge, you should be ashamed of yourself for attempting to besmirch the man's integrity and reputation."

"He defiled my child, his reputation be damned. His integrity is already lost. Sir." Rachel began to walk away from the gathering.

"Stop! I will order them to shoot."

Rachel and Catherine slowly melted into the soft greens, whites, and yellows of the vast empty meadow, but the commander stayed all weapons.

Beatrice leaned toward the commander, careful to hunch her shoulders so that her bosom pressed out of her bodice. When she had the commander's attention, she lightly placed her open hand on the commander's thigh and whispered, "Give us one day sir. Allow us to convince the girl, speak sense to her. One day will cost you nothing, but may gain you everything." She slowly removed her hand from his thigh, "Either way, I'll be waiting."

"Please sir, take this to your men on our behalf." Barbara smiled and offered a small sack of tea. "We do not want war, and we do not wish suffering on your men."

The commander stood abruptly. "You will know my answer by sunrise."

His detail picked up the bag as the commander walked away. One of them whispered *thank you* to the ladies.

The commander ordered the perimeter guards signaled in and gathered his lieutenants. "We are remaining posted until sunrise tomorrow." The lieutenants murmured. "Silence. We will end this in the morning. Prepare your ranks and then report to my tent for dinner service." The commander faltered but caught himself. The lieutenants did not notice.

Thaddeus grabbed a lieutenant leaving the commander's tent. "Where is Catherine?"

"Mr. Monroe, please return to your tent. We are standing down until sunrise." The lieutenant brushed past Thaddeus.

"Sunrise? Why are we waiting another day? Lieutenant. Lieutenant!"

Scouts rushed back to the camp one by one, and all reported their checkpoints deserted. Points three and six found stacks of bodies, freshly split from stem to stern with some sort of large knife.

The lieutenants rushed to the Commander's tent. They opened the flap and ducked as the Commander's desk chair flew past their heads and into the muddy field.

"You will not take me, demons! Wait...wait...Who are you? What is that? Oh no, no, please, I didn't mean to, no, please why are you doing this, why? why?"

The commander flopped on his temporary desk screaming in agony, writhing and trying to escape unseen claws until he heaved and fell to the ground. A lieutenant approached the commander's limp body carefully.

"I think he's still breathing, but barely. And his heart, I cannot tell if he is still with us." Within the hour the encampment mobilized.

The lieutenants ordered the tea destroyed, but by the time the order made it through the camp, a handful of officers had succumbed to the poison.

Within an hour, scattered gunfire and the screams of soldiers struck by whatever the Connors had at their disposal, rang through the dense bayou. In all, the family kept the soldiers at bay for nearly eight hours.

Once the battalion was able to set fire to the back of the house, checkmate was not far off.

Rachel and Catherine emerged from the burning building. Rachel was cut down from the fence line and soldiers poured into the yard. Two men grabbed Catherine by both arms and pulled her into their custody while the remaining soldiers flanked the house and covered the front and back entrances. As the Connors tried, one by one to escape the flames, the lieutenants' soldiers took aim and executed them.

Pleasant D. and Sarah remained inside the inferno, their cries coursed through Catherine's veins and the blood of her unborn child.

When the troops returned with Thaddeus' prize, he was beside himself. "Catherine, my child, I am so happy you are safe."

Catherine shrugged away and would not embrace Thaddeus. His countenance hardened, "So be it. Child, you belong to me, and you will one day appreciate what I've done for you."

Thaddeus made it known in Johnson's Bayou that he cared for the "honor and safety" of the newborn child and her mother, and would therefore "take Catherine's hand in proper marriage and raise the child as his own."

Catherine whiled away the years of her child's infancy and adolescence in silence. She tended to her daughter, whom she loved in spite of her father's crime, and to her beautiful garden of exotic plants.

When the Great Storm of 1886 ravished Johnson's Bayou, Catherine made her escape and left the child behind. Thaddeus did not hunt her down. She had served her purpose in his life by granting him another child, and he longed to spend his time in younger arms.

SUNDAY

14

"Hello? Lara? Hello? Answer me!"

Lara held her cell phone to her ear. "Yes, I'm here."

"Christ Lara, I thought you were dead! I've been calling all day."

"I am quite alright. Now. Yes, I'm better than ever, you could say."

Lara had spent the better part of Jean-Baptisté's absence sitting in the dark. With each sleepless morning's arrival she awoke, bare and shivering. For a moment she would permit herself the fantasy that she'd wake above her condition, and that the sinewy madness that paralyzed her would subside. Instead she would pour a drink and sink back onto the floor to stare blankly into the darkness and wait.

"Security destroyed my phone, I apologize for being incommunicado for so long, how are you? I miss you so."

"As I said," Lara answered mechanically,"All is well. When will you be home?"

"In two days, I am flying into LAX at nine PM, do you want to pick me up..."

Lara interrupted him, "Excellent, I will be waiting for you at home. Goodnight."

Lara set her phone on the ground.

Jean-Baptisté stood in the soft, District of Columbia rain listening to a silent line.

"Jean-Baptisté, did she answer?"

"Yes. All appears to be well."

"I'm glad to hear that."

"Agent Hensley, why am I here?"

"To serve your country."

"Specifically. Why am I here?"

Hensley moved under an overhang and lit a cigarette. "There's no meeting with headquarters. I brought you here on my own."

"There's no job?"

"There's definitely a job. And the benefits are outstanding. You'll just be working for me first, and the United States second."

Agent Hensley offered Jean-Baptisté a cigarette and Jean-Baptisté refused. "A colleague of mine believes your apartment building is home to a few high level members of an anti-American syndicate."

"Terrorists? On Spring Street?" Jean-Baptisté smiled, "I know you guys are good at what you do, but you're wrong on this one."

"We need to know for sure. We need eyes and ears, intel, reports."

"I'm never home, and when I am, I'm with Lara."

"This is where your charm comes into play m'boy. We have two dozen of these," Hensley held up a nickel-sized surveillance camera. "You just need to talk your way into the right places, drop a camera, and let us do the rest."

"For the United States."

"If that helps. Yes."

MONDAY

15

Above the city's star-muting skyscrapers, pulsating branches of lightning mingled and coursed through the low rumbling storm clouds. Sheets of dense white noise dropped violently from the skies above. The streets were empty—a brief weekday reprieve between the rush to drink and the rush home.

Pershing Square was amply populated by displaced persons sitting, walking, and in various forms of sleep and/or rest. All soaked, all completely exposed on a dreary summer night—some with the ability to go home, most, with no such luck.

Keagan crossed Grand Avenue and pressed on with his cap pulled down and his overcoat pulled tightly against his thin, soaked frame.

Dire frustration broke the silence—

"Fuck! Fuck you, you fucking fuck!"

"Cadence?" Keagan looked across the street and saw a huddled figure assaulting a trash receptacle with a pair of dirty green steel-toed boots.

Keagan rushed across the perilous rivers forming in the gutters along Sixth Street. "Cadence!"

The huddled form continued kicking, "Cadence! Cadence, is that you?"

The form looked up; her clear blue eyes glistened above a black silk scarf covering her mouth. "It is you, what the fuck are you doing?"

"Go away Keagan."

"Seriously, have you gone mental?"

"I said fuck off Keagan."

"Tell 'ya what. I'll step over here and you can have it out with the rubbish bin as proper violent as you like. Then, you are going to join me for a poolside drink at the Hotel Figueroa, rain and all." Keagan smiled.

In spite of herself, Cadence smiled; she was pleased she had thought to wear the scarf over her face. "Fine, keep walking, I'll catch up."

Keagan tipped his cap and the raindrops formed a veil over his smile.

As he crossed Hope Street, Keagan heard her victorious cheer, "Fuck you! Fuck. You. Bitch."

Keagan turned and walked backwards. Cadence jogged to catch up, "Mr. Keagan, what a surprise, let's have that drink shall we?"

"Everything's okay?"

"Mind your own business, fucker."

The Hotel Figueroa was practically abandoned. Stern and ornate columns rose sixty feet above the earthen-tiled floors. Blues, pale reds, and greens created a halo around immense braided skylights crisscrossed in black iron—anchors for heavy, latticed chandeliers levitating in the warm lobby's sky.

Beneath these Olympian heights, low sofas choked with large, decadent cushions framed the court and dissected the south wall into comfortable sitting rooms for semi-private conversation or concentration.

"This place is really incredible, somehow I've never walked in," Cadence confessed to the ceiling.

"Really? That's a crime. Take your time, look around. Unfortunately, they haven't had a busy night in years."

Cadence was lost in the detail on every wall, every surface, and every temporary fixture. "Someone loves this place." Cadence stroked the dull metal antiques.

The rain beat powerfully against the blackened glass of the skylights, and Keagan became impatient, "Hey, it's raining pretty hard, let's get that drink."

The bar was drenched in low, red light. North African divans of fine velvet and black lacquered wood were draped along the wall, and two-person tables sat silently in formation beyond the bar. The patio looked out into a cascading symphony of clapping raindrops and rough, idle concrete. The brightly lit pool seemed to hover in darkness, changing its perimeter to shadow. Reaching cacti of bulbous, phallic, and alien proportions crowded the walls ringing the courtyard. Small, subtle spots lit the beds of succulents and created a constellation of tiny stars behind a wet, cyan sun.

Keagan leaned childishly against the bar with his hand on his cap brim. "Nice eh?"

"Yes. Where is my drink Keagan?"

"Oh, well, I didn't..."

"Two stouts, whatever you have," Cadence flipped a twenty-dollar bill at the scruffy bartender. The bartender left the money on the bar, swung once, and set two uncapped beers in front of Cadence with a sly smile.

Cadence laughed, "Nice trick."

"Thank you. Anything else I can-"

"Nope, but thank you." Cadence demurred, wishing silently that flirtation was not pain, but every time her skin warmed, she felt ill. Without Orin, everything seemed a hollow endeavor.

Cadence met Keagan at the edge of the bar's canopy. "Shall we?" Cadence asked.

"Yes. The bartender seemed to be getting a little friendly."

Cadence looked Keagan in the eye. "None of your concern."

"True. I'm sorry, I was just trying to help."

"Well don't. Being female doesn't make me your responsibility."

"That's not what I meant."

"There are three billion-plus men on this planet. Every single one I meet tries to get into my pants at some point. So, Mr. Seward Keagan of the Revision Program, what I'd like, is to be treated like a human. Not as the gatekeeper of a vagina."

Cadence stepped off the short tiled patio and the pair entered the symphonic, minor deluge.

They found semi-dry seats beneath a battered umbrella.

The immense coffin-shaped blue lagoon was pocked by kamikaze raindrops—each taking aim and penetrating before the crystalline surface repaired itself and returned to its state as barrier to the depths. Glass pin drops animated the colorful tile table surfaces and danced in chorus with the drops perishing against saturated seat covers.

"This is one of the best places in Los Angeles to sit when it rains." Keagan smiled as he looked up into the white raindrops falling beneath the spotlights surrounding the Staples Center. "And the Library. Of course."

"What about it?"

"That's another place, Central Library is brilliant in a rainstorm."

"I imagine that's quite lovely, the whole ceiling being glass and all."

"Precisely. There is also a bridge that moves between the Literature and Fiction sections on L3. It puts you as close as possible to the Atrium's ceiling, where shadows dance beneath passing cloud cover and crashing rain drops."

Cadence smiled, "You love the rain Keagan."

"You have no idea."

"Why Los Angeles? Shouldn't you be in Seattle?"

Keagan smiled and lit a cigarette. "You can never know when something will become too much of a good thing. If I moved to the Pacific Northwest and realized that my lust for rain had everything to do with its absence, I'd really be fucking myself."

"That's a very complicated excuse."

"Thank you," Keagan bowed and hid his lighter in his jacket pocket. "New York is too expensive, Chicago is inextricably stuck in Illinois, and leaving the country hasn't been an option for some time. I needed buildings, a city, so, here I am."

"Well, welcome to the city that never was."

"Slainté." Keagan raised his glass.

"Your mom." Cadence smiled and clinked her bottle against Keagan's. "What time is it Keagan?"

He reached for his phone, "Um...130 ante meridian."

"I'll be back. Do you want another on my way?"

"Absolutely, I'll hold the fort." Keagan adjusted the table's large umbrella.

"Okay, you do that." Cadence pranced out into the rain, tip-toeing expertly across the tops of puddles ringing the pool.

Quite agile Keagan thought, staring unconsciously. *Oh no*, Keagan considered for the first time that he might have a wee crush on Cadence. "No, no, no," Keagan admonished himself and lit another cigarette. *That's a super fucking bad idea.*

The rain began to steadily lighten as the night slipped away. Keagan watched the bartender washing glasses, stocking shelves, and answering an archaic landline telephone complete with an extendable metal antenna and no internet capabilities. His scruffy appearance was a polished and contrived hat tip to personal conformity and a deep desire to see said conformity in those around him.

Purposeful apathy, be it hygienic or social, spoke to such a wide spectrum of Americans that it simply made no sense to call these phenomena trends. *Trend* infers impermanence and what we were staring down the barrel of was a good old-fashioned social evolutionary change. This contrived front became the latest addition to the canon: preceded by (in order) the opposable thumb and the bi-cameral mind.

Keagan felt a bit judgmental. What could someone like Cadence see in a guy like that? Could a slick hipster lure her in? Surely not, Keagan decided, but she had seemed flattered by his clumsy bar trick. Keagan began to feel a little nauseated, he was jealous. He sucked back his pint and lit another cigarette.

"Hey," Cadence snapped her fingers a third time. The bartender flashed his late-night sitcom smile. *Ugh*, Cadence thought, *I'm really sorry I offered to get the drinks.* "Um, hi, yes, another round, por favor."

"Right away miss," the smirking bartender tried his best to maintain eye contact as Cadence spun on the barstool to face the pool and Keagan's shadow—occasionally lit by a small orange circle of burning tobacco.

When Cadence turned back around the bartender was waiting, still and silent, with all teeth bared in stilted seduction.

"How much do I owe you?" Cadence retracted, hoping to sarcastically, lightly telegraph just how creepy El Barkeep was getting. After all, provoking ignorant cocksure males tended to be the path of most resistance.

"A lifetime of devotion and constant access to those gorgeous blue eyes."

Cadence wretched. "Look, whatever your name is..."

"Josh," Josh attempted to hold Cadence's hand.

"Look fuck-o, get your hands off me before I break those delicately manicured fingers."

Josh pulled away.

"Excellent. Now walk over to the register and make change for my friend and I and we'll be done with all of this petty awkwardness." Cadence smiled, she desired no static.

Josh walked to the register mumbling.

Cadence called out, already knowing the answer. "What did you say, bitch?"

"I said you're a tease, chatting me up and then acting like I have AIDS."

"Chatting you up? Tell me Josh, which part of our miniscule, tedious exchange did you consider provocative? Would you have construed that sub-par volley of human interaction so special if I had a penis?"

"No, what? I'm not into dudes." The bartender looked around, wary of who heard him shriek in defense of his heterosexuality.

Oh fuck, Cadence thought, *it's a bigot too.* "You make me sick." Cadence left the bartender three pennies for a tip. "Choke on it, asshole."

She walked rapidly out into the courtyard and set Keagan's beer in front of him before shaking her hands and arms off.

"This rain is supposed to stop at two thirty." Cadence grunted.

"It seems like it's calmed down considerably." Keagan offered.

"Salut," Cadence lifted her bottle and clinked it against Keagan's.

"You look very nice this evening." Keagan offered sincerely.

"If by nice you mean fully hosed off and ready for a shower, yep, I'm crazy-nice!" Cadence laughed and lit a cigarette.

"No, I'm serious, you look very nice. I've always thought so." Keagan paused; *fuck, I went too far.*

"Keagan? Is there something on your mind?"

"No, no. I mean, no."

"Look Keagan, I'm not interested in your half-assed advances, capisce?"

"I get it. Besides, looks like you're more into the scruffy-haired bicyclist type."

Keagan tried to shove his words—punctuation over consonant—back into his idiot mouth.

"Fuck you Keagan. I hope you die in a fucking fire. As in, a fire on your fucking face, starting somewhere near your ass and crawling toward your ignorant mug."

"Whoa. I know I deserved that, but whoa."

"Change the fucking subject."

"Sure. What do you have against trash cans?"

"I saw a rat."

"And?"

"And it's my singular mission on this planet to exterminate rats."

"Okay?"

"It's quarter after two, I need to run two more errands before I call it a night."

"Cadence, I'm sorry about---"

"Are you coming?"

"Where?"

"You're such an asshole Keagan."

"Oh right, yes, I am. Let's go."

"The rain stopped." Cadence looked skyward. "This may still work."

"What?"

"Fewer questions, more hurrying."

Keagan followed Cadence into the dark, cold night. The subsiding storm left the air downtown still, and dead. The pair owned Figueroa and shared it only with the fabled vermin Cadence could not suffer living.

"What's the deal with the rats?"

"What do you mean?"

"They are foul creatures, and a trustworthy sign of decay, but you...hate them."

"Don't confuse fear with hate. I don't hate anything, it's a waste of energy."

"You have a tendency to disagree with how I say things more than what I'm actually saying."

"And?"

"Why the fear? I'm curious."

"My parents had a white kitchen, white tile, white floors, white grouting, towels..."

"Okay, got it, white."

"...my father laid out a steak, a fine cut of meat, something he was looking forward to. As he was turned, preparing another part of the meal to come, a mid-sized rodent pressed its smug little snout against the steak. My father swept his hand across the handle of a large hammer, and brought it down repeatedly on the conniving rodent. Our pristine, spotless kitchen was transformed into crime scene in seconds. Thick, dark blood creased the tiles and grout. By all accounts the surface had been the scene of a particularly nasty and excessive massacre, and guess who had to clean it up?"

"That's a brain teaser."

"We were not meant to share the planet. And I'm not going anywhere."

"I can certainly understand your general disdain. I understand arachnophobes quite well, but you seem so laissez faire with everything else."

"What are you afraid of Keagan?"

"People. Especially lots of them. In the same place. Touching."

Cadence smiled, *of course.* "Imagine with me what it would be like: the sight of a crowd, it's shadow, lighting across fouled asphalt. It's jerky, scavenger gait, inducing immediate and uncontrollable rushes of anxiety and nausea—gut wrenching existential-style surrender."

"Sure, I get it. And my misanthropy was in no way amplified by childhood horror like yours, but don't you have to *live and let live* at some point?"

"When does tolerance become capitulation? At what point is decorum appeasement?"

"They wish you no harm."

"Bollocks." Cadence bent down and placed a small shoebox beneath a bush alongside Pershing Square's south perimeter. Several feet across the silent sidewalk lay a shame-encrusted City of LA Department of Sanitation bin with adjoining bag and slatted cradle. Home to *them.*

Cadence rushed Keagan along by his arm.

"Hey, Cadence, we're going the wrong way."

Cadence bolted into the park and drug Keagan along.

"Shut up Keagan, there's a car following us, it's been following us since the hotel."

"I haven't seen any cars..."

Tires squealed outside of the futuristic park's perimeter wall. Cadence pulled Keagan into a tiny cubby between wall and bench and dropped to the ground. Keagan joined her and she watched the park for movement.

"There," Cadence pointed to the northeast corner of the park. A long black Crown Victoria crawled past the break in the barrier at the staircase. Cadence heard the car come to a slow halt and two doors open and close.

"Come on Keagan, let's split."

Keagan and Cadence sprinted from the park as two chaotic flashlights crawled every surface and joint of Pershing Square. When they had safely crossed the street, Cadence pulled Keagan into a short alleyway on the south side of Sixth. A large, forgotten marquee floated above the urine soaked, rubbish-strewn road to nowhere.

"I want to see who these fuckers are." Cadence hunkered down.

"That's not a bad idea," Keagan pulled a cigarette from his pack and Cadence slapped it out of his hand.

"Are you insane? You might as well use a mirror to signal them, or better yet, just stand up and start yelling *fuck the police*."

"No, no, you're right, my bad."

"Here they come. One's an old stereotype Dick, and the younger one looks like he probably had a *Miami Vice* poster on his wall in the fourth grade. What time is it Keagan?"

"Two minutes until three."

"Most of the primates have filtered out of the bars and are headed back to South Park and Spring Street."

"So?"

"So, it's time to teach them a lesson."

"The college students?"

"The vermin. Please place your hands over your ears Keagan, this isn't going to be pretty." Cadence receded between her hands and was penetrated by a deep and satisfying smile, expectant of all wishes fulfilled, all grudges collected upon.

She's going to blow them all to hell, Keagan panicked.

As Keagan placed his hands over his ears, the younger officer flashed his light into the alleyway.

"They're down the street." Detective Idi Koboko yelled to his wheezing overweight partner, "I'll meet you there."

"Wait you bastard, wait for me---" Detective Oliver Worecester's plea was eclipsed by a sudden and pervasive crackle, hiss, and then silence. Worecester and Koboko both froze and looked skyward. Beginning in the distance and moving rapidly down Fourth, Fifth, and Sixth Streets a parade of explosions proceeded east from Figueroa. Both Detectives hit the ground after the third explosion rang out; both had their hands threaded over their heads when Pershing Square's receptacles blossomed in a monsoon of multi-colored confetti and rubbish, clouding the inky sky with color. As the tiny strips of innocuous paper rained to the quiet streets and sidewalks, Cadence grabbed Keagan's arm. "Come on fucker, let's get out of here."

"That was..."

"Yeah. It sure was. Those rats will think twice about setting up shop in this neighborhood. Let's not wait around for those pigs to come to their senses."

16

Jean-Baptisté's plane descended during a rare thunderstorm over the Los Angeles Basin. The passengers had circled LAX for almost an hour and the natives, as they say, were getting restless.

"Ladies and gentleman, I am happy to announce that we have been cleared for landing." The pilot's voice was greeted by loud cheers and revelry.

The herd moved toward the baggage carousels slowly, defeated. The anxious hour spent in the air had destroyed the passengers' good will and the collective excitement typically associated with arrival.

A man in a chauffeur's get-up approached Jean-Baptisté. "Mr. Baudron?"

"Yes, who are you?"

"Mrs. Baudron sent a car for you. I recognized you right away, she said you'd be handsome, but, *wow*." The driver composed himself. "Right this way Mr. Baudron."

The driver placed Jean-Baptisté's luggage in the Town Car's boot and took his place behind the wheel. "Ready sir?"

"Yes, thank you." Jean-Baptisté answered distractedly. His time in DC had been very intense, but Jean-Baptisté wore the smile of a contented man. His host accepted him as a viable and valuable candidate, and they began discussing methods immediately. Jean-Baptisté returned to his ladylove with a new purpose in life. Finally, he would be more than captured light. Finally, he could make his father proud.

The long black car stopped in front of the Spring Street Lofts. Jean-Baptisté tipped and dismissed the driver. The front desk guard greeted Jean-Baptisté gushingly, "Welcome back!"

"Thank you, it's grand to be back." The silver metal elevator doors parted and Jean-Baptisté rushed skyward to the ninth floor. The marble hallways felt closer, dirtier. The echo of shoe heels and verbose conversation made him instantly pine for the utter silence and remote escape of the suburbs north of Washington DC. He couldn't wait to tell Lara that this messy, violent, and compassionless city would soon be safer, all due to her husband.

His keys slid into the lock and the heavy front door pushed open with a click. The loft was dark with the exception of several dozen candles strewn chaotically about the main room.

"Where are you my love?"

"Welcome home Jean-Baptisté." Lara whispered from shadow.

"Lara." He turned, startled. "Where..."

"Here my love." Jean-Baptisté's eyes adjusted to the blackened room. Lara was sitting, back straight, hands in lap, waiting in a large leather chair near the loft's bay of levered windows.

"Darling...why are you sitting in the dark?" Jean-Baptisté approached his obsession and his one-true joy. "The candles are beautiful. Come here I have missed you, I don't want to be away from you ever again." The couple embraced, but Jean-Baptisté could feel the chill in Lara's shallow, and inconsistent breaths. He could feel the chill in the apartment, the stasis of death. Lara's head was tucked into his shoulder; her tearless, blank eyes faced the empty darkness of the loft.

"I missed you too." She finally answered.

"I have a very big surprise for you Mrs. Baudron," Jean-Baptisté smiled and began to walk toward his luggage. "But first, I am dying to wash that stifling flight off my skin."

"Take a shower, I'll unpack for you, fix you a drink, and be waiting."

"I am truly home." Jean-Baptisté beamed as he kissed his sullen wife on the forehead and disappeared into the bathroom.

The scalding shower filled the room with steam; Jean-Baptisté did not notice that Lara walked in. When he stopped the flowing water and the curtains of cottony-white steam receded, he saw his wife leaning against the sink's pedestal, exposed, with the exception of black silk stockings, garter, and heels. Jean-Baptisté smiled and began to dry off while Lara set his drink on the counter.

Jean-Baptisté kissed her slowly. Her lips were pensive, had he been gone too long?

Lara pulled away. "I want to watch you shave." Her eyes awakened, a pale flame, and her lips curved into a dangerous smile.

"There you are." Jean-Baptisté grinned compulsively, his precious wife had returned. "Maybe not so many Xanax, eh?"

She flattened against the wall as Jean-Baptisté moved to the sink and slipped his heavy silver safety razor under warm water. She watched him carefully strapping the blade, setting his mug and brush in the same place he always had, mixing the white cream carefully and thoroughly. She admired his long, articulate fingers, their blithe indifference to opposition, and the way in which his body commanded objects, rather than succumbing to their fragility. Jean-Baptisté expertly spread the soft cream on his face and Lara's eyes narrowed in anticipation. Her heart began to race as he pulled the metal edges across his strong jaw.

Jean-Baptisté recognized her fidgeting, "Everything ok, my sweet?"

Lara did not answer. Jean-Baptisté waited with the razor hovering over another section of unmolested white billows.

"Yes, sorry. Quite, alright."

Jean-Baptisté smiled ignorantly and drew the blade against his skin once more. The cavern of exposed skin ended in a small, bulbous prick of bright red blood. Lara smiled, *It is done.*

Mrs. Baudron crossed the bathroom floor and embraced Mr. Baudron from behind. He relaxed. Whatever had been hiding between them when he arrived was now gone. He had his dearest hope, struggle as she may with that role, and he would soon be the husband she deserved.

"Lara, the surprise...I have something very important to tell you..."

Jean-Baptisté lunged forward and dropped the heavy safety razor into the porcelain sink. Lara tightened her grip on his torso and buried her tears into his naked back. Jean-Baptisté's eyes widened in horror and he bucked powerfully against the pedestal, screaming at his reflection in the mirror and weeping uncontrollably. His distended lips formed no words, only agonizing guttural gasps until he dropped to his knees and Mr. and Mrs. Baudron collapsed to the ground.

Together, at last.

Lara tenderly ran her fingers through Jean-Baptisté's hair as he lay lifeless on the bathroom floor. His eyes were absent as the dead.

TUESDAY

17

I'm just hearing things.

Keagan tucked his hands between his knees and kept his eyes on the floor in front of his doorway. He saw shadows rushing back and forth, a feeding frenzy of negative light drawing closer and closer to his door. Keagan looked away, afraid to face the shoddy wooden barrier. The footsteps became louder, bouncing off every surface of his bare sub-terra box—flocking, fluttering, and menacing like a murder of black-winged messengers. Keagan clutched his eyes and ears, the sound threatened to overwhelm him—then silence. A friendly knock shattered Keagan's protective cocoon.

"Hello?" He called out weakly.

"Hey weirdo, it's me."

"Dave" Keagan sighed. "Come in man. It's unlocked."

"Hey, didn't mean to startle 'ya." Socialist Dave pushed open Keagan's door and made a beeline for his desk chair. "I wondered if you were up for a pint. Then I realized I never got your number."

"Yes, some company sounds perfect right now."

The pub on the corner of Fifth and Spring Street was hosting the SoCal Rollerderby Association's end-of-season throwdown. Kneepads, black eyes, and weaponized ponytails filled the booths and bar, turning a timid Tuesday night into a rager.

Kuraš watched the shenanigans from the bar, the last vestiges of a dying scene, strangled to death by development and kitsch. As university sweaters and ten-thousand dollar pets began to replace safety pins and wasted youth, the money set the culture. Money culture always tamps down compassion because compassion listens and money dictates. To listen is to choose engagement, and to dictate is to impose silence.

"Kuraš. It's good to see you."

Kuraš turned, "Jacob. Can't say the same."

"I'm glad age hasn't softened you up. Thank you, by the way."

"Don't mention it. Ever."

Kuraš raised his hand and wagged two fingers. The bartender nodded.

"Well, well. Locals get preferential treatment I see. Is it safe for us to talk here?"

"Nothing you and I have to say is more interesting than thirty drunken athletes on rollerskates."

"Then you know why I'm here."

"Yes. You're apparently some sort of high-functioning narc."

"I figured you'd see it that way. You're not much for subtleties."

"Nothing subtle about snitching for the Feds."

"They had me on some old shit, and I knew a guy who knew a guy. The whole thing was a setup, make some anarchist kids look bad, make 'em think twice about raising hell during important meetings."

"Yeah, that sure worked out."

"I wasn't part of the A team. We were still at the warehouse preparing for the protest when the first shop windows were dropped. Next thing we know cops storm the warehouse and make a big show of destroying the place. It was the first in a long line of operations."

"Ok, so you're a narc *and* gullible."

"If you say so Kuraš. I didn't have a choice."

"You had a choice, you just couldn't make the right one."

"Same old Kuraš" someone caught Jacob's eye. "Since we're already reacquainted, I'm going to go make a friend." Jacob clapped Kuraš on the shoulder and headed toward the back of the bar.

Jacob approached a klatch of powerful Derby goddesses who were curling their fingers—sirens beckoning Jacob's rickety skiff onto the reef. Kuraš watched as he bowed to them and began to make animated small talk. The goddesses closed in on him like the supple palate of a flytrap. Kuraš signaled, and a pair of Derby Gals restrained Jacob and skated him out the back door without kicking up a speck of dust. The rest of the bruising beauties smiled at Kuraš in chorus.

"Done and done."

There was a long silence between Keagan and Socialist Dave.

"Ah, I forgot, I'm responsible for instigating conversation with you."

Keagan tilted his glass in acquiescence.

"You look pale, shaken up, what gives?" Socialist Dave did not mince words.

"Nothing much, just losing it." And neither did Keagan.

"Like classically *losing* it, or like strange smells and clouds of black flies coming from your apartment *losing it*?"

"The former. I had always imagined that insanity would present itself visually, like I'd start seeing things over my shoulder in the mirror and such. Peripheral madness. But no..."

"Still voices?" Socialist Dave interjected half-heartedly.

"Sort of. I mean sometimes, but mostly, it's so clear, just boots."

"Like demonically possessed boots with forked tongues and designs on your mortal soul?"

"No fucker, I'm serious. Boots. People using the staircases, usually the one leading to the back corridor. People afraid of being heard, people scared of something much larger and far more vicious than they are." Keagan looked past his stout and into a small sliver of mirror duct-taped to the wall facing the bar. "They can't be real, but that doesn't stop me from trying to find them."

"Find them?" Socialist Dave perked up.

"Sure. Sometimes I even leave the studio and follow the sounds."

"And?"

"No one."

"Ever?"

"Ever."

"What happened tonight?"

"I waited, and more came, some going up to the surface and some coming down. I walked onto the landing and, as usual, there was no sign of human beings anywhere. Then I heard a door slam. You know how the doors in this building slam. Anyway, I couldn't tell which direction it came from. I tried every door on the floor before giving up. As I walked back to my apartment I heard the boots again, scuffling slowly, carefully. I stopped and listened to the sandpaper symphony of stolen steps. That's when I knew."

"Knew what?"

"That I'd lost it. Like classically. It was not a dream, I was not drunk...well, not traditionally drunk. Yet here was a clear auditory hallucination with no end."

"So..."

"So I walked back to my apartment. The boots sounded like they were slowly following me from covered positions in the hall. I shut the door behind me, sat on the bed and closed my eyes, hoping the hallucination would just go away."

"And then an even bigger pain in your ass showed up!" Socialist Dave laughed and took a deep swig from his pint.

"Frankly I was glad to hear a real voice. There's no one down there, right?"

"Sorry Keagan, just you."

"Right. So, what brought you down to my purgatory?"

"Something Kuraš said a few days ago. If you had the chance, to change the world, would you do it?"

"I doubt it."

"Why?"

"I pay an inordinate amount of attention to one thing: me."

"Christ, you're bundle of sunshine. There's plenty of change going around and this country is due for a large force-feeding. Our duty is to one another, always, and right now that duty is disrupting tyranny as often as possible."

"To what end?"

"To the ultimate end: peace and prosperity for all."

"Limos, yachts, and implants?" Keagan assumed.

"Food, clothing, and time to think, play, and create."

"I appreciate your goals."

"It's one AM, we'll be drunk soon, so let's have it. Are you some sort of covert government project?"

"Why would you say that?" Keagan became nervous that the suggestion made too much sense.

"Well, you are *special*, to someone. They locked you in a basement at the center of a particularly nasty gentrification battle, and now you're hearing invisible army men."

"That's pretty paranoid, but still, it sounds like I ought to rethink the plot of my book."

"Fucking homerun that is, I expect royalties."

"I think you distrust anyone who shaves daily and wears suits on purpose."

"Maybe. It's just hard to run from the cops when you're dressed for a job interview."

Keagan pulled up his trouser leg and showed Socialist Dave his steel-toe boots, "Cadence inspired me to get these. There isn't much I run from."

"Well, holy shit, basement boy has teeth after all. Maybe it's your absolute silence on political matters that makes me nervous."

"I learned a long time ago that long-term relationships don't mix with politics."

"Lost some friends did 'ya? You should meet Kuraš."

"Quite a few, but good riddance. I just don't buy the idea that people want Big Brother, they've been seduced into thinking it makes them safe."

"You're an anarchist."

"No, anarchists have a positive outlook when it comes to humans. I want to be free, but not because I think I deserve it."

"Fair enough. What about the benefits of a government that works for the people?"

"I think it's a grand idea, but there's no evidence that it's a functional concept in the long term."

"Humanity is already hardwired to cooperate. We are pack-animals after all."

"Peaceful dispute resolution is where Nature falls short. As beasts, our primal and final solution is violence. As thinking beasts, we figure out how to turn that violence on others."

"The powerful turn it on their subjects."

"The teacher on the student."

"So there's no Keagan-sized solution?"

"Of course not. But that also means that laws, and borders, and war, are not the solution."

"So get rid of 'em."

"Exactly."

"Maybe you're right, but until then, we have to save as many lives as we can. Once you are in those zip ties you run the risk of being written off as a *sympathizer* and disappeared."

Keagan tilted his pint. "The best bet is to be heading out of this lopsided country. I plan on making tracks as soon as this book deal pays off."

"How's that going?"

"Well?" he replied weakly.

"Sorry I asked."

"I wish it was complete, I'd be off."

"To?"

"Probably Ireland."

"Ireland's still in pretty bad shape."

"Exactly, I plan on being cheap immigrant labor until they tell the IMF and EU to fuck off."

"Well, if you find that magical window *out* you be sure to let old Dave know, eh?"

"No offense, but if I find an out, I'm going through it. Quietly."

"Kuraš! Who were you talking to? He looked a little square..." Josh/ Mike mocked from behind rather large non-prescription glasses. His thin, waxed mustache seemed pasted on his upper lip.

"My ex-cellmate from prison."

"Cellmate? There is no fucking way that you've been to prison. What for?"

Kuraš leaned in, "Shut up you little prick, I don't really need you broadcasting it. I had a disagreement with a cop over his job."

"Well, that's a bullshit answer. You don't go to prison for disagreeing with a copper. Arrested sure, beaten, sure, shot, definitely, but prison is a stretch."

"Depends on the disagreement. Assault got tacked on late in the game to ensure I did some time."

"So lay it on me, old-timer. What happened?"

The bar was a din of half-finished conversations. Kuraš turned to the young hipster, "It was all over a stop sign.

"The stop sign in question rested stoically in front of a two-level office complex, the area was rife with them. Anyway, I had been scared into completing my associate's degree-"

"Wait, scared?"

"Yes. I was a rookie with the City at the time. One morning I went toe to toe with one of our project managers over permit scheduling. He pulled rank and I inferred that it was a cowardly move."

"Inferred?" Josh/Mike asked dramatically.

"Fine, I reminded him that there is an *enormous chasm between doing what is right and doing what is convenient.* He was confused by my use of *chasm* rather than the easier, and more convenient *gap.* I terminated the call and immediately began fretting over my lack of a degree, my lack of upward mobility, and finally, my lack of job security. Again, this is of only minor importance-"

"Minor?"

"Stop interrupting me, especially if you insist on doing so in single sentence questions."

"Sorry. I like to break your rants up with questions about minutia. It's a little game I play to convince you that I'm paying attention."

"Where was I?"

"Didn't earn your AA, pissed off a VIP, now your A-S-S is G-R-A-S-S. And, go..."

"So I signed up for art school that afternoon. Expensive, and unfortunately non-transferable, art school. They offered night courses so I could continue working. For almost two years, after a day's duties and wondering when I would get the old boot, I drug my bones to the art school.

"I'd walk to the coffee shop during our school breaks to see different faces than the ones I was trapped with throughout class. One night, as we all lit cigarettes and tried to decompress in fast-forward, I noticed a cop using the school's parking lot as a hiding place. He was waiting for people to run or roll through the stop sign directly in front of him on the street. I was immediately pissed, I mean, that's shady."

"Very."

"Right?"

"Totally." Josh/Mike reaffirmed.

"I thought, fuck that guy, this is private property. I smoked my cigarettes and eyed the officer as we walked past his car. I stopped short of approaching him or provoking him with obscene gestures. After all, I was twenty-five at the time, too old to flip off a cop and have it written off as *cute*...it was difficult though."

"A little bird is nothing between citizens, eh?"

"Assault, if they want to push it. You know better than that."

"I just meant."

"I know exactly what you meant."

"Fine, carry on, oh Oppressed One." Josh/Mike flicked his wrist dismissively.

"So I watched this bastard parking in the school lot once a month, looking for easy victims. Finally I approached the administration about it. They thought I was insane."

"Um...*insane* may have been a little too kind."

"So I appealed to the school board requesting that they provide an opinion on my submission: *Police Use of Private School Facilities for Unrelated Operations and Monetary Gain.* I was nearly dismissed from the school."

"Big surprise. Seriously man, pick your battles, right? The coppers are gonna knick 'ya anyway, there's no point."

"No point? That's what's wrong with you Josh/Mike."

"It's. Joshua. Michael. You fuck."

"The point is that unless we resist, they will occupy our every waking moment. Complacence kept people from asking *why* when our nation's police forces began to purchase heavy machinery and military weapons for everyday activities. Through the nineties and after the millennium, tanks, helicopters, chemical weapons, tasers, crowd dispersion, subversion tactics, *enhanced* interrogation, and provocation became publicly normalized when used on US citizens."

"And protesters."

"Yes, especially protesters," Kuraš' eyes wandered the room. That evening would likely be the last time he wasted money at the corner dive. "When we close our eyes, we lose our ground."

"So, this fuckin' cop is camping out and popping the peeps as they roll past." Josh/Mike tried to keep Kuraš on track.

"Yes, shady."

"Right. Correct."

"After trying the proper channels I decided it was time to take matters into personal consideration, e.g. direct action."

"Whoa, like sabotage? Nails in the driveway, or foamy shave cream bomb on the windshield?" Josh/Mike was visibly agitated and dying to hear some violence or drama.

"Better."

"Yes, lay it on me man."

"I liberated a sheet of high-density, art-school-grade poster board from the graphic design room and made a sign. *C-O-P* and a large arrow pointing to my left."

"Oooo, nice, but a bit drab, eh?" Josh/Mike was offended by Kuraš' lack of style.

"You'd think."

"I do think."

"I marched out to the stop sign and I hoisted it in front of my chest so that approaching cars would hit *C-O-P* and arrow with their headlights in time to react to the warning. Several cars passed, coming to safe, sane stops and flashing their lights in gratitude. The officer finally looked up from whatever was so drastically compelling in his lap. I watched him looking me over, trying to determine what I was doing, standing on the sidewalk with a sign. After some time he opened his squad car's door and placed his baton on his belt.

"'How are we this evening?' He asked as he approached. 'Excellent, officer, and yourself?' I responded. 'May I ask what the sign says?' I turned so that the police officer could read the rudimentary missive as I waved to another car honking in support.

"'I see. That's pretty clever.' He smiled, but I thought it unwise to respond. 'Let's move on though, I'm conducting police business and you are interfering.' He was very calm, a young officer, probably not yet fearing for his life or jaded by the aforementioned fear.

"'With all due respect sir, I'll remain where I am.'"

"Oooo, I bet he didn't like that." Josh/Mike was suddenly interested again.

"It didn't bother him; he smirked. 'What do you hope to accomplish here?' He asked me, sincerely I think, but with a hint of petulance. I told him that, 'I hope to save people some money while increasing the efficiency of the stop sign.' 'Very admirable,' he smirked again, 'but that's not your job.' I told him that I disagreed, that my job as a citizen was also to protect and serve, but 'hiding, like a swollen spider, to generate revenue for city was beneath his calling, and frankly, an insult.'

"He didn't see my point. 'If people run this sign, their safety is compromised. By citing people who run this stop sign, I am creating a deterrent.' I told him that I agreed, however, 'I take issue with the methodology. I am performing the same function, arguably, in a more efficient and less-punitive way. There is, however, one glaring difference.' 'Which is?' he wanted to know. 'No money is changing hands.'

"He wasn't impressed, 'Fines are a great deterrent. People who pay a hundred dollar ticket remember that for a lot longer than a guy with a sign.'

"'Perhaps, but more importantly fines make certain things possible: uniforms, training, helmets, batons, weapons, power. Without lust for power, there is no need to do any more than hold a sign.'

"He considered this for a while. He tried a line of thinking that painted me as a vigilante, but I assured him that *vigilantism seeks to change the direction of power.* My aim was simply to help. 'By unloading some of your burden—yours specifically, officer—I hope to lighten the overall burden of the police department. With concerted effort toward this goal, we could all conceivably witness a day when we need only a fraction of the standing army we have patrolling our streets in police uniforms.'

"He asked me if I advocated robbing the police department of revenue, to which I replied, 'Yes! Precisely. Local and state funding would be sufficient to manage a reasonable police force. Without revenue generating capabilities, police departments would be forced to hire and train only the women and men necessary for the job (which should be primarily administrative anyway) and get rid of the heavy artillery, chemical weapons, and Pentagon liaisons.'

"'That will cripple law enforcement.' he decried, 'Nonsense,' I replied, 'it would force them to respond to crime, REAL crime, instead of running political, para-military, Homeland Security, and DEA operations at the behest of rich patrons and/or the US Government.'

"He didn't give it a moment of thought, he seemed to have already made his decision, 'Okay, I can appreciate your desire to help, but right now you are interfering in police business,' his demeanor had changed, 'so please vacate the sidewalk.'

"'I am on a public sidewalk officer, with all due respect, I will remain here.' He dropped his head in resignation. 'I am asking a final time.' 'I am refusing again.'

"He removed his handcuffs and pulled my hands, one at a time, behind my back. Click, click."

"Shit." Josh/Mike whispered into his Blue Ribbon lager.

"Yeah. Only time I've ever been arrested."

"What happened? You can't stop there!"

"Why not? That's the best part."

"Fuck you Kuraš, what happened?"

"Nothing much, the station had a good laugh at my expense. I couldn't keep my mouth shut and ranted for several hours re: the corruption of a militarized police state and its inevitable ill effects on the children of every officer within earshot. Somewhere along the line assaulting a police officer got tacked on to my charges and I spent a year in prison."

"That sounds like the best part. You're a pathetic story-teller." Josh/Mike turned and ignored Kuraš.

WEDNESDAY

18

Cadence fell into Hank's from a warm, grey morning, and shook silent raindrops from her newly shaven head. A hunched man at the far end of the bar paid unwarranted attention to her entrance. Emmy approached from down the bar and crossed her arms as she asked Cadence what she wanted to drink.

The signal meant Cadence had come out for nothing. So she comforted herself with bourbon neat and stared intently at a small turtle flailing in a dirty aquarium behind the bar. She had nicknamed the small reptile "Strug-Knight." By the time Strug penetrated the water's surface via a slick, plastic dock, he would slip again and sink carelessly to the bottom. By the time he appeared *settled* he began his struggle to the surface once again.

The hunched man rose from his stool and walked toward Cadence.

"Please keep walking, please keep walking...shit."

"I've seen you somewhere before haven't I?"

"I doubt it." Cadence kept her face forward, it was the stereotype Dick from Pershing Square.

"You're probably right. I'm thinking of someone with a long ponytail, unnatural greyish color. You could be sisters though. Anyway, you have an awfully nice smile, you should use it more often." The man pulled a stool out next to Cadence.

"Don't get comfy, asswipe, and don't tell me what to do."

"Woah, woah, woah young lady. Feisty is nice, but lets not get personal."

"What do you call giving me instructions on what to do with my face?"

"A misplaced courtesy. Are you sure we've never met?"

Emmy nodded at the man, *he* was her concern.

"Look, no one is buying that combover, and if you touch me, you'll draw back a bloody stump."

"This used to be a cop bar. Seems like it's gone to hell."

"Emmy," Cadence called to the bartender, "Get Detective Worecester whatever sludge he was guzzling when I walked in, and put it on my tab." Cadence flipped the officer's wallet onto the bar and it lay open, showing his badge.

"That could get you in a lot of trouble missy."

"Not likely."

"Oh I get it now, you're one of them downtown cophaters, right? Was your lesbian lover collared with the rest of the traitors?"

Cadence turned slowly. "You watch your mouth, flatfoot."

"Ah, I struck a nerve. What was her name?"

"I never have and never will consort with pigs. We just don't run in the same circles, it'd never work out."

"Here's the thing, precious. I *do* like that smile. Enough to do a little something for your jailbird pal."

"Too late. He's dead, scumbag." Cadence nodded to Emmy and stood.

"You know, people like you get to play Big City down here because of people like me. This isn't the kind of neighborhood that's safe for, you know, young vulnerable girls."

"Been down here ten years Worecester, you're not talking to a silver-spooner."

"Then don't come crawling to us when someone finally straightens you out, *missy*."

"Get fucked, *Olly*."

19

—American Leaders reflect on the Liberation of Libya

"Bullshit. That should read, 'US usurped sovereignty of fifth non-hostile government and still pays no price.'

—Former Secretary of State expresses Sympathy for Egyptian Protestors

"Shame she and the President have no sympathy for Americans being beaten and gassed for protesting against our corrupt government."

—Law Enforcement Officials discuss the possibility of using Drones to Police American Streets: less harm to law enforcement in-theater, discussing processes for fitting less-lethal weapons to crowd-control drones

Kuraš threw his coffee mug across his empty studio, "Fuck! What will it take, robot police officers? This country is so far up it's own ass, I don't know...wait..."

—IAEA Report being used by Anglo-American coalition to justify a military assault on Iran

"Not this again. This President may actually have the opportunity to start this war. We're all fucked, kiddies. Bend over and kiss your ass goodbye."

Kuraš walked down the long ramp leading to the sub-terra parking garage beneath the Alexandria Hotel feeling the effects of his strenuous night out.

The Alexandria's parking attendant, Renalto, was always happy to see Kuraš. Renalto was the sort of hardworking chap that always smiled. Eight AM with a stack of angry power-yuppie hipsters waiting to go to work: smiling. Three AM as the same examples of carbon-based-waste trickled drunkenly from the neighborhood pubs, bars, and snark-fests: smiling.

"¿Que pasa, Kuraš?"

"Nada, amigo. ¿Como esta?"

"Bien, bien, where you going today?"

"The Valley."

"Oooooo," Renalto affected fear.

"I know, nothing good comes out of a trip to the Valley."

"Today is different, yes?"

"Yes. I certainly hope so my friend."

Cadence claimed there were rats running amok beneath the Alexandria: *Walking slowly, insolently toward holes in the wall near useless traps that the fat vermin mock.* Kuraš had not seen a rodent in the garage, but the filthy walls, collections of liquefied rubbish in the corners, and lack of sunlight struck Kuraš as the prettiest picture one could paint of a rodent Valhalla. Kuraš situated himself behind the small steering wheel of his car and flipped the Long Beach University jazz station on.

As Kuraš crested the long ramp out of the garage, he slowly applied his brakes and looked into the mirror on the wall above his car. He was clear to the right, as he looked left a man and a woman crossed his path. The man held his hand in front of him and walked sideways, unsubtly shielding the woman.

Kuraš couldn't help himself, he leaned out of his window, "Oh fuck, it's a good thing you're here, without your authoritative hand, that poor woman would have died beneath the clawing axles of my powerful American automobile."

The man looked back for a moment, out of pity for the elderly man shouting gibberish at him.

"See mom," he whined, "it's dangerous down here, people are insane."

Kuraš hoped for a fixie-biker to scare, but the Mayor's gaudy, fluorescent green, Super-bikelane was—as it seemed constantly to be— empty.

Once down Sixth Street and onto Main, Kuraš ran aground on an unnatural reef of stranded cars. "What the fuck?" Retired and off-duty LAPD in uniform and hazard-yellow vests stood garrison protecting a film crew and their attending vicarious masses. Downtown was rife with pick-up motion picture and television shoots, fashion spread obnoxiousness, and the occasional deadly and ill-conceived construction project. The cranes heavy with cheap lights and the mass of cold, shadow-encased extras, made it clear: television magic was being made.

"Fuck, fuck, FUCK." Kuraš beat various parts of his steering wheel, door, and radio. Kuraš had nowhere to be, not really; that wasn't the point. The City of Los Angeles' unquestioning fealty to the movie industry (in all of its infant- through retirement-phases) spat in its citizens' faces time and time again. *We cannot fix parks, roads, or education this year. What we will do instead is completely dedicate resources to nullifying your ability to traverse an already paralyzed city. All for a little extra paper on the side.*

Kuraš reached the light at Fourth Street thirty-seven minutes and fourteen seconds later. Before his silver Dodge could penetrate the intersection, two uniformed officers entered the roadway and held their hands aloft.

"Now what?" Kuraš growled.

The officer on the left glared through impossibly reflective sunglasses and brandished a bright silver duster-style mustache and awkwardly stylish calfskin motorcycle boots. The younger officer nervously looked back and forth between the line of cars and an invisible cue to hold the morning commuters at bay. He had no boots, the younger officer, as he had arrived by squad car. He didn't have a mustache either, but that seemed to be an old-crackery-redneckey-cop sort of thing anyway.

"Hey, people have to get to work," Kuraš leaned out of his window and shouted.

Neither officer responded.

Kuraš honked his horn and held his hands up in the standard American *what the fuck?* expression. The fancy retired cop held his hand higher, as if the inch or two in elevation would suddenly wrest Kuraš' anger to the ground.

"You have got to be fucking kidding me." Kuraš looked around. People laughed and gave him thumbs-up. *If they're holding up traffic,* Kuraš reasoned, *then they are probably trying to get a perfect shot.* He laid on his horn and looked around at the other cars, asking for solidarity honks.

The young police officer broke rank and approached Kuraš. A chorus of car horns—short and brisk, long and obnoxious, frequent and infrequent—broke through the morning pall and drowned the early morning commute's apathy in collective civil disobedience.

Kuraš smiled broadly, "Take that, you fucking bastards."

The confused centurions received a cue to let the cars pass. The commuters all rushed to freedom honking in congratulatory bliss. Kuraš' smile faded as he crossed First Street and passed the former Occupy Los Angeles encampment. Oppression poisoned the ground and the grass refused to grow. *Fitting,* he thought.

On the way back from cleaning out his stash in Van Nuys, a city that Kuraš had long reviled, he parked near Cahuenga and Ventura and walked on to an English pub to wait for a message. Kuraš eventually cracked open a worn publication of Chomsky essays regarding Latin America and US Intervention during the nineteen eighties. A handwritten note fell from inside the cover:

Basement Boy is clear.

20

Keagan heard whispers, rhythmic, sanguine missives. There was no hint of peril, no causal alarm, so Keagan listened. Attentive, seduced, and undeterred by the slow erosion of time—no nod of acceptance, nor scowl of discontent, only captive, kept, and coddled by the soft, billowing words. The voice stopped; pax et silencio.

Keagan leapt from his bed and flattened against his wall; the room's darkness consumed.

"Who's there?" Keagan shouted into the darkness.

Serious bare knuckles rapped the door—seriously. Two combat boots obscured the meager light spilling weakly beneath the front door.

"Open up bitch, we have shit to do."

Keagan opened the door. Cadence stood on the landing in a FUCK the LAPD t-shirt with a thin, zippered hoodie over her arm.

"Ah, hello—I love your shirt—I had a lot to drink last night...well, this morning, and I don't know if I'm up for..."

"Nonsense. Get dressed, I'll wait. We're riding the subway and a few buses, so dress comfortably." Cadence flipped on a lamp and jumped in a chair.

"Did you shave your head?"

"No." Cadence kept reading a small, stenciled pamphlet.

"Are you sure? You definitely had a ponytail on Monday."

"Okay." Cadence had already lost interest.

"Right, okay."

"Nice boots." Cadence paused. Keagan was wearing a tweed flatcap, jeans, and a t-shirt. "I've never seen you so *dressed down*."

"Comfort, you mentioned comfort."

"I almost forgot. Here's a bagel. You're welcome."

Keagan smiled. "Thanks, but I'm more of a coffee-for-breakfast sort of guy."

"Eat a solid breakfast so you can run from the cops."

"Are we going to be running from the cops again?"

"You never know."

Cadence herded Keagan through the chaos on the sidewalk. By the time Cadence reached the Pershing Square subway entrance, Keagan had lost her by half a block.

"Keep up. I'll leave you where you stand."

"I didn't even want to come."

Cadence stepped onto the down escalator and began to disappear beneath Hill Street.

Keagan followed.

"You're working on a book right? How's that comin' along?"

"I still have a problem with disappearing pages, but I'll sort that out."

"The ghosts downstaaaaaaiiirs..." Cadence made a spooky wind-through-the-barren-branches-sound and widened her eyes.

Keagan laughed, "No, the ghosts are just trying to convince me I'm mad, no biggie. The missing papers, they could cost me everything. I need to get out of that basement, sane or not, that is my priority."

"Won't you miss all of us?"

"Sure, but I won't be moving to Pluto."

"The planet, or the former planet?"

"The planet."

Cadence smiled, "Good answer. What about the forces of evil swirling about in the basement?"

"Fuck them. If they want to tromp around all night smoking cigarettes and listening to punk music, who cares. They seem to be committed to staying unseen, so I don't expect any knocks at my door—live and let live."

"That's very tolerant of you."

"I'd say non-confrontational. Realistic."

"Realistic, unless there are ghosts."

"There aren't."

"There's something."

"Fuck Cadence, whose side are you on?"

"Yours Keagan," Cadence smiled. "This is our train, *North Hollywood*."

Cadence waited politely for the passengers to disembark before she pushed in and snagged two empty seats facing the ADA-reserved seat.

"I met Dave."

"I heard."

"He invited me to come up to the apartment and work. When the voices get bad, I mean. I think it will do me a heap of good to breathe less-than-fresh air through large windows. If that's kosher with you, I mean."

"It is." Cadence answered stoically. His feeble attempt at an ingratiating humility put her off, ever so delicately.

The exposed viscera of Los Angeles rushed past in utter darkness—whipping across the plastic windows, hurtling ahead into an unseen chasm.

"Look out there." Cadence pointed toward the front of the train. The tunnel ahead was bathed in enough artificial light to see the snaking tracks as they rose to the Wilshire/Vermont platform.

"That's pretty fucking cool." Keagan kept his eyes on the track ahead as the train pressed on, deep beneath Vermont Ave. and rushed north toward Sunset Boulevard.

Cadence watched Keagan's nervous tics; he wanted very badly to be doing something *else*.

"What are you thinking about?" Cadence asked abruptly.

"I'm sorry?"

"Don't be."

"Um" Keagan stammered.

"Look, there's no wrong answer, I'm just curious."

"Well, I was thinking that a cigarette would be nice, which slowly devolved into wishing I had slipped a notebook in my pocket. Then a brief internal argument over the merit of trying to type an idea into my phone—as opposed to writing it on my forearm---"

"Or asking if I carry paper—I do."

"Really? That's fantastic. That's all I was thinking, for the record." Keagan scribbled whatever was left of his thought.

"Okay, we're coming up on the end of the line."

Cadence led Keagan up to the surface, and across Lankershim to a deserted bus terminal on the edge of a massive turnaround lot. She seated herself in the abandoned station and motioned for Keagan to do the same.

"No thanks, been sitting for a while now."

"Sit down, asshole."

Keagan complied.

"Now, slowly, look up and to your right, then left."

"Why are there nine police officers standing about in a bus terminal?"

"Because the LAPD is understaffed," Cadence spat. "The more you draw attention to yourself, the worse off you end up, capisce?"

"Aye. That's our bus over there isn't it?"

"It is."

"Let's go."

"Not until the driver comes around."

"But he's just sitting there, he's not even taking a break."

"I've never met anyone who could have a problem with everything in the universe simultaneously."

The Metro Orange Line consisted of a long snaking bus-highway cut through the 'burbs of North Hollywood, Van Nuys, Reseda, and Canoga

Park. The grim, arachnid station at Van Nuys Boulevard was devoid of life. Across the platform, resting on bike racks, squad cars, and benches, a line of navy blue authority eyed Keagan and Cadence warily.

"Keagan, I said no eye contact, get with the program."

"Sorry, I just don't understand why there are so many cops at the bus stations."

"Ticket dodgers."

"Wait. Seriously?"

"Well, that's the Party line on the subject anyway."

"What about turnstiles, gates, cameras?"

"Make no mistake, they have cameras everywhere. They are monitored in real time, and if you so much as set a skateboard down on the platform the disembodied voice of the Metro-god comes over the loudspeakers to reprimand you."

"I found that out the hard way."

"When the underground was first complete, there was no fear of ride hopping; it was difficult to get anyone to ride the thing, period. Then the sinkholes caused by subway construction shredded Wilshire Boulevard..."

"Wait, what?" Keagan asked.

"The City began digging beneath Wilshire near the tar pits, and the surface gave way. Massive sinkholes replaced large swathes of Wilshire Boulevard for miles. The Orange and Red lines draw a sort of perimeter, on one side lies solid bedrock, and to the south and west...sand sand sand."

"Bad place to dig tunnels."

"None of the affluent neighborhoods would sign off on elevated trains. Eventually the communities on the route south toward Long Beach were coerced into accepting the Blue Line stretching from Seventh and Fig downtown to the harbor in Long Beach. Slowly commuters began using the trains and the City saw their opportunity to capitalize on punitive fines for unpaid fares. Now we have chipped metro-passes.

"Enter the Final Solution: Sheriff's Department personnel at the North Hollywood station in the mornings, then evenings, then afternoons as well; they had scanners and checked each ticket and chipped-card one at a time, creating frustration, bottlenecks and the inevitable dragnet of *that guy isn't supposed to be in this neighborhood, let's search him*. Boots on the ground creating their own war out of sheer boredom."

"Imagine if all of those resources were pointed at solving and preventing actual crimes."

"Hard to imagine. It's never been that way."

"I don't know if you can say that." Keagan pressed.

"Law is the protection of private property. By extension and by purposeful contrivance, *offense to property* becomes *offense to person*. The State pits each citizen against the other by deign of a perpetual need to protect yourself from everyone else's *freedom*."

"I heard about Dave's solution, what do you think we should do?"

"I'm not a utopian, I'd rather focus on the enemy in front of us. We need to burn this thing down and in the process discover a saner way to conduct our civilization. Until we all understand the con, we'll only find small-scale solutions for exclusive groups. Violence succeeds because it needs no marketing campaign."

"You don't expect to see the end of this, do you?"

"No. Do you?" Cadence walked between the small, two-story, brick buildings comprising the pulsing shopping centers around the intersection of Van Nuys and Victory Boulevards.

Cadence stopped in front of *Poco Vestidos de Princesa* and finished her cigarette.

A long black Crown Victoria rolled to a stop across Victory Boulevard from *Poco Vestidos de Princesa*. Detective Worecester put the car in park. "I couldn't get over the way that little bitch talked to me."

"Why didn't you cuff her, make her calm down?"

"I can't, asshole. Ever since that *incident* in Boyle Heights, I can't so much as make a surprise visit. But I looked her up anyway."

Detective Koboko feigned interest, he knew better than to dissuade his partner's insane rants. "Okay, and?"

"Shut up, here she comes."

"I don't see...oh Oliver, the punk rock kid? We have better things to do."

"She set those explosions on Monday. She's also Orin Lynch's wife.

Koboko looked puzzled, sorry for Worecester.

"Cadence Lynch, the anarchist psycho that got little Bobby Sarconne tossed from the force."

"What? That looks nothing like her."

"She shaved her head, idiot. Got rid of her courtroom clothes. That bitch was relentless. Bobby was gonna be a great cop, just like his Pops. He didn't deserve what happened, she just wouldn't let it go. After she mentioned her ex at Hank's, I realized God had given me a shot at a little justice for Bobby and his Pops."

"Her ex? The man's dead Olly."

"Fuck her, fuck him, and fuck you. Don't call me that."

Detective Worecester's partner, Idi Koboko, tended to employ a practiced sympathy as his part of the continual good cop/bad cop dialog. Koboko also knew how to dress. Although he hailed from a *dirt-poor, god-fucked, third-world hell-hole* according to Worecester, Idi owned two suits for every day of the week. They weren't *nice* suits in the traditional sense, but he treated them with as much respect as a retired general treats his beloved ribbons.

Cadence approached the dressmaker and they had a short, whispered conversation. The women disappeared behind a dirty crimson curtain hanging in a doorway behind the cash register.

Keagan stood still, *what the hell am I supposed to do?* He walked between the redwoods of taffeta, glass diamonds and butterflies, purple chiffon, black ribbons and white silk. The full, plump skirts rubbed against one another blocking egress as Keagan sank deeper into the rainbow forest of dresses. His view of the register and the front door eclipsed, the ceiling gave no clue regarding direction. Keagan began to panic; each empty gown gave way to a new row of empty gowns. He pressed through dress and dress-stand alike until he emerged in the clear aisle bisecting the small shop.

Fuck this, I'm going back outside.

Keagan stood on the sidewalk and lit a cigarette. He caught his reflection in the empty storefront glass next to Poco Vestidos de Princesa. He barely recognized himself out of slacks and with his head covered by a cap. The seemingly abandoned left-door neighbor to the dress shop was stark in comparison. The lively reds, yellows, and greens of Poco Vestidos ceased at the structural wall and were replaced by a dull and forgotten steel grey with black, desiccated, wood trim. There were no official city or county notices taped to the windows, and Keagan could see no sign of painter's tarps or construction. *Abandoned*, he concluded.

Worecester embarrassed Koboko. He did not understand America. He did not understand Uganda, either. He could not understand most things about most places, but he could put his suit on every day and represent the free peoples of the world—sleeping deeply every night.

"That shady fucker in the cap was with her on Monday night." Worecester growled.

"You're not jealous are you?"

"I swear, one of these nights there's going to be an ugly shootout and you aren't going to make it..."

"What do you intend to do, Detective Worecester?"

"I'm going to find out what she's planning and put an end to it."

As Keagan held himself up against a parking meter, his eyes were drawn skyward by movement on the dress shop's transom window. A long black car came to a slow stop across the street behind him. He couldn't see anyone inside the vehicle, and the bright sunshine turned the car's windshield and windows into an array of large curved mirrors. Keagan watched the car nervously. The driver's side window slowly descended and stopped abruptly at half-mast.

Keagan dropped his cigarette. *Fuck.* He bent down to pick it up, blew on it, and continued to smoke.

"He made us," Koboko whispered to Worecester.

"No way."

"Get us out of here, I'm telling you."

"Shut up Koboko, or so help me."

Keagan came to the end of his cigarette. He could not decide what to do: if he turned to confirm the strange images in the window was he giving into insanity? Keagan crushed the cigarette on the heel of his boot and placed the butt in his pocket. *Okay, I have to know.* He looked up; the long black car was gone. He spun around. No cars were parked on the street, as if a street sweeper had washed them all into the rain gutters.

Keagan decided to walk back into Poco Vestidos. As he approached the entrance, the creaking door opened.

"Keagan, come on let's split." Cadence walked past him and continued silently south on Van Nuys Boulevard.

"Hey, hey!" Keagan called after Cadence. "What the fuck is your problem?"

"Don't have one, Keagan. You're not in very good shape are you?"

"I'm not in *bad* shape, I can still see my feet every morning. I'm just used to walking mutually as opposed to playing catch-up."

"My apologies, we are in a bit of a hurry now."

"Where did you go?"

"I needed to speak to someone. Now I need to drop a note off to a friend."

"Any chance we can have something to eat along the way?"

"Definitely. After we drop the note off, we'll have some lunch and a pint or two. Deal?"

Keagan was easy. "Deal."

The snaking Ventura Boulevard trek from Universal Metro Station was grueling. With the sun raining violence between storm clouds a jacket was too much but bare arms, similarly, were untenable.

Cadence stopped in front of a store that had littered the sidewalk with large mirrors positioned near the ground on flimsy aluminum easels. "This seems dangerous doesn't it?"

"I'm getting progressively hungrier." Keagan tried to smile through his newly throbbing headache.

"He's here." Cadence whispered to Keagan as she grabbed his hand and pulled him close. Stand still and pretend to be shopping for mirrors." Cadence stared into the mirrors one at a time, like a director. "Have you met Kuraš?"

"Kuraš? Doesn't ring a bell."

"Older guy, smokes too much, rants about politics and hipsters down at the corner pub. He lives in the building."

"I did hear an older guy school a college freshman on American military-interventionism recently."

"That sounds like Kuraš. Look in the center mirror. The man in the green and blue Pendleton behind the pint of stout is Kuraš."

Keagan narrowed his eyes, "Yep, that's him. Let's *not* say hello."

"Agreed." Cadence tightened her grip on Keagan's hand. "I just need to leave him a message. Anonymously. In case anyone's watching."

"Watching?" Should he tell Cadence what he *thought* he saw?

Kuraš rose from his seat and entered the small English pub.

Cadence sprinted across Ventura Boulevard. She scribbled something on a piece of paper retrieved from her back pocket and slipped it into a book sitting alone where Kuraš was enjoying his pint. Cadence rushed back across the busy thoroughfare—more carefully this time—and leaped via aerial onto the curb from a few feet into the last lane.

"Hai!" Cadence lauded her perfectly stuck landing with a short exhalation.

"Very impressive."

"Gymnastics. Shall we go?"

They walked at a serious gait toward the Universal City Metro Station.

"So what was that all about, Cadence?"

"Nothing."

"That's pretty shitty. I do have a massive hangover you know."

"Something is going on with Kuraš. He's old, he's stubborn, and he doesn't take very good care of himself. I need to know that he is okay. I am a mother, as you know."

"That's right. Why haven't I met your, son?"

"I don't introduce every headache I meet into his life. I'm not creating any black holes in my son's heart when someone up and leaves."

"Or dies."

"Fuck you, Keagan. Fuck you right in the neck. The State won't let me see my son."

"Because of Orin?"

"You're a super genius, congratulations."

"Sorry Cadence."

"You keep having to say that. A little prevention goes a long way."

21

The alley-view balcony of a snobbish Scotch bar on Seventh Street played empty concert hall to Will & Liam's incessant debate. Inside, the warm bar hummed with conversation, colliding billiard balls, and the subliminal din of college radio. The low clouds from early in the day had kept the City in a blanket of summertime chill: crisp, static-laden cold that kept Will & Liam alone on the dark balcony.

"Cock."

"Rooster." Liam answered, unamused.

"Man-Hen."

"Rooster." Liam repeated.

"Whatever." Will grunted into his pint glass.

"No, not *whatever*," Liam, in his mind, slammed his fist on the table. "Fucking fix it."

"Rooster. So…"

"So, this Rooster has a problem, eh? Something he can't quite tackle alone. So he meets a lady hen…"

"…She-cock."

"Are you four years old?"

"Sort of. I assumed that was why they stuck me on the project." Will continued sketching a female counterpart to their proud-combed protagonist.

"He wakes up one day and the world has changed."

"Has been destroyed," Will adds amidst strong, dark pencil strokes.

"Destroyed? It's a kid's book man, that's a little extreme, don't you think?"

"I guess, how about completely pitch dark?"

"Tough to see, no room for Seussian visuals; keep trying."

"On fire."

"San Francisco nineteen hundreds, or fires of Hell?"

"Maybe Hell. Our Rooster lives in a deep valley..."

"He rises, to hopefully ascend into some sort of peace?" Liam continues.

"He does it for a girl."

"A hen." Liam reminds his partner. "Wait, wait wait..."

"What? I am loving this, he wakes up to flames, where is his She-cock?"

"That's basically *The Divine Comedy*." Liam pushed his hat across the booth and flipped his arm onto the back rail.

"Oh. Well, fuck."

"It's too dark anyway."

"Sure, I guess. What about a mythical creature in a large hat that kidnaps children for adventures? Then returns them just in the nick of time before their mother gets home?" Will offered.

"Did no one read to you as a child?" Liam asked with pity.

"No. Why?"

"I like the cock...fuck...Rooster, let's stick with him. Right. So a Rooster wakes up..."

"Cock wakes up."

"Do you two mind?" Lara asked as a tiny circle of orange fire illuminated her face.

"Not at all ma'am, pardon us." Liam tilted his head. He had not seen the breathtaking woman in the shadows; she had already smoked one cigarette and was using it to light another.

"Thank you." Lara held her third 50-year-old Glenfiddich aloft and continued to smoke in silence.

"By Zeus, did you see the young lady good William?" Liam gushed.

"William? Why did you call me-"

"She is exquisite, I cannot take my eyes from her. It's embarrassing."

"You got that right. Hey, focus."

"I can't talk about cock anymore, not now."

"Give me a break."

"Madame, may we ask for your help? We have a creative quandary and fresh ears would no doubt make all the difference."

"No." The woman answered carelessly.

"You see," Liam continued undaunted, "we are collaborating on a children's book, a picture book, illustrations, and well, we're stuck."

"I said no," The stunning apparition would not budge.

"She said no," Will reminded Liam.

"Very well, I apologize," Liam adjusted his vest and tie before turning back to his drink. "Shame," He muttered under his breath.

"What if the Rooster meets a sloth?" Will offered.

"A sloth? Why?"

"Sloths are lazy, Roosters are early risers, it's the archetypal dichotomy for Capitalist children."

"That's a terrible idea," Lara spoke while staring into the amber fluid at the bottom of her tumbler.

"Why is that?" Liam wanted to know.

"That Capitalist spiel made me ill."

"Well, *thanks* for that," Will said, "but we have work to do."

"She's right." Liam was mesmerized.

Lara looked up for the first time and crushed her cigarette in an ashtray. "May I join you gentlemen?"

"Of course," Liam stood immediately and offered Lara his seat.

She looked Liam up and down, more as a warning than a greeting.

Will was lax and unconcerned.

"You know," Lara addressed Will as she took Liam's seat, "if you took a razor to that hair you'd be a damn good looking man." Her smile resonated heat.

Liam took his seat next to Lara in the short booth. His mind was paddling desperately on a sea of mixed signals.

"So, lovely-lovely-lady, no sloth. Will. Will? Hey, Will?"

"Yeah?" Will didn't look up from his sketch.

"Cease any sloth-like sketching, just scratch it out, roll it up, and throw right into the rubbish" Liam barked at Will, who continued to ignore him. "What do you suggest my sweet mysterious stranger?" Liam held out his hand, "I am Liam, by the way," and gestured to Will, "this is Will,"—still sketching.

Lara ignored Liam's hand, "I prefer bunnies. You'll see a lot more Bunny-Chicken relationships in the real world than chicken and sloths."

"Too true," Liam beamed.

"Cock." Will corrected, eyes on paper.

"Rooster," Liam blushed.

"So this Rooster, he's a meany," Lara smiled for the first time, "a hulking, grey bird...and he's a farmer."

"Okay, okay, and he grows" Liam tried to interject.

"He's not generous, he's very stubborn and wants all of his farm to himself. One day a soft young bunny with mud on her little feet skips into the farmer's orchard and discovers resplendent multitudes of ripe, juicy fruits."

"Okay, okay, and the Farmer" Liam tried again.

"The little bunny—innocent of such coarse things as property—has several berries from a low bush. After taking a moment to savor the fresh juices dancing slowly over her little bunny palette, she scampers off into the forest drunk on forbidden berry juice." Lara made suggestive motions mimicking sticky sugary juice running down her neck and across her chest.

Liam's eyes nearly dislodged from his skull.

"But, what about" Will looked up for a moment.

"Silence!" Liam shouted. "Please, continue."

"Lara."

"Ah, luscious Lara, charmed. You know, I once knew someone na---"

"The Farmer finds his orchard in disarray. Well, disarray meaning that three single berries are missing from one of hundreds of trees—and decides that the world is unsafe for his plump, precious pieces of perfect pulpy delight.

"The farmer builds an immense wall and begins to hunt the tiny bunny with the help of a small swatch of fur the bunny left behind on a barbed-wire fence." Lara's arms illustrated the Bunny's unfolding saga. "But there are consequences. The Farmer's wall prevents sunlight from reaching his precious plants so some of them begin to die. While the Farmer is out hunting, he is not tending to his spoiled flora and they begin to wither in jealousy."

"This is getting a little dark don't you thi---"

"For the love of...*shut up* Will." Liam was exhausted, utterly confused by Will's behavior. "Continue, Bella. Please."

"Soon, there is no farm to defend, no farm to stake his revenge on, and the Rooster becomes mad with obsession, flaying all creatures in his path," Lara's hands dropped between her thighs and she began caressing them through her skirt, "until the Bunny is brought to justice."

"Right," Liam stared, choking on his words, "the Bunny, dead, right."

"No, no, no, what the fuck is wrong with you?" Will raised his head and Liam was signaling him to *cut it out*. "What? What's wrong with you Liam? We have a book to finish, we can't afford to break into chaos every time some pretty girl-"

Lara was surprised. "You think I'm pretty?"

Liam grunted quietly, "Let's let the lady finish her thought."

"Whatever." Will went back to sketching.

"So the Bunny, won't take this shit lying down, she's a special bunny. One day the forest animals ask her to help them, protect them from the Farmer..."

"The Rooster." Will interjected.

"Correct. So she makes a special potion from leaves in the far off Silent Bayou. She invites the Farmer to attend a tea, during which she will give herself over to him in exchange for the safety of the forest's animals.

"The Rooster agrees and the date is set. The entire forest gathers to watch, safely out of sight. As the Rooster cautiously approaches the small table, the Bunny sits and pours tea for two.

"The Rooster hovers menacingly. 'You stole from me. You are the thief that has caused all of this.'

"'Yes sir. I apologize. Please allow me the honor of serving you tea before I turn myself over for judgment.' The Rooster nods and seats himself. The Bunny lifts the cups and hands one to the Rooster.

"'To trust,' The Bunny toasts. 'To justice,' The Rooster snuffs and scrapes the ground with his claw. The Bunny and the Rooster finish their tea silently. 'Soon,' begins the Bunny, 'you will taste the sweet warmth of justice.'

"'I prefer *now*.' The Rooster removes the Bunny's head with his razor-sharp beak.

"He looks around at the animals in the treeline, waiting for one of them to attack. No one moves. As the Rooster begins to stand, his long, proud legs wobble. As he attempts his fourth step, the immense grey bird collapses to the ground.

"The animals rejoice and play in the Farmer's garden, eating berries, bathing in its rivers, swinging from large, fruit dripping apple and orange trees. The mad Farmer, the Rooster, hangs from an immense oak, in a trance—under the Bunny's spell—his face blank of expression, forced to watch his secret protected garden used freely, decadently, by all."

Lara paused.

"It's a story my mother used to tell me."

"Fucking genius." Liam had settled into Lara's grip.

Will looked up, "You have got to be kidding. Eviscerating the Bunny? Magic potions and a zombie Rooster? Anarchy as an end to brutal means? This is not what we are working on."

"Yes, yes, you are quite right. Look, lovely Lara, I think it's simply too obnoxious in this place to continue such a delicate conversation." Liam looked at Lara conspiratorially.

A cricket somewhere deep in the alley chirped, "Um, it's pretty quiet out here" Will mumbled.

"Come to my place." Lara uncrossed her legs so that Liam could see her bare, silken thighs.

"Yes, that's perfect."

"Well, I guess that's it." Will began to put his tablet away.

"Let me see what you were working on," Lara asked sincerely.

"It's not done."

"Please?" Lara did not try flirtation with Will, he didn't seem to be biting.

Will flipped his sketchpad and propped it up behind two table candles. He confessed, "I'm going to hit the pisser," and walked back into the bar. Lara placed her hands on the edges of the sketchpad and adjusted the candles. Liam dropped his head in defeat and sat back with his arms crossed. Artists are able to charm in moments, a scribe must tender seduction with stamina.

The pencil-sketch concerned a young girl with Lara's eyes reading a large, overflowing storybook. The characters—a large, ominous Rooster; a soft, wise-looking bunny (fluffy as you please); and forest animals—in trees, in patchwork homes full of love, and finally under attack—spilled from the immense book onto the bottom half of the sketch. The waterfall mural told the story of the mad Farmer and the conniving Bunny.

"It's breathtaking," Lara whispered.

"Like you."

Lara shrugged Liam off and pressed out of the booth.

"But I thought"

"In order for *that* to happen, you'll need to convince your friend to join us. Here he comes, bonne chance."

THURSDAY

22

Three of the nine basement apartments in the Spring Street building opened on a cement common area forty feet below street-level. Stale raindrops pulled from their moorings on the windows above and crashed against the silent concrete. The top of the great chasm squeezed the expansive California sky into a box, robbing it of its majesty.

Cadence pulled a door shut behind her. "Let's make this quick, Basement Boy is out and about."

Kuraš yawned. "Good morning. The guy I brought down to the corner bar was a Fed narc. The team will leave him tied with a ribbon in the basement for the authorities. We have a friend wearing the narc's tracker and pretending to be busy on the roof. Needless to say, we had to speed up the plans for the evacuation, it's happening tonight during ArtWalk. We're running point on the building. Word is we need to keep our distance until everyone is out of LA. After that, we're on our own. I got your note that the guy in the basement was OK'd by the Dressmaker."

"Shouldn't we warn him? Keagan, I mean." Socialist Dave asked.

"No way."

"He's going to get mixed up in the aftermath, Kuraš. He doesn't deserve to be collateral damage." Cadence insisted.

"Do whatever you like, once we are clear. Not before. People's lives are at stake, let's try to stay focused on that."

"Of course, forget I mentioned." Socialist Dave conceded.

"I'll run crow's nest from my apartment. Dave, we need you down near the pub. If they come, they'll roll down Spring Street, and we'll need a heads-up. Cadence, we need you in the alley behind the building in case I'm wrong and they approach from Main Street." Kuraš smiled. "Try to enjoy yourself, we're actively subverting our corrupt government. And probably ruining ArtWalk as a bonus."

23

Keagan checked his post box infrequently. He knew as well as the next person that checking the mail was a violently disappointing experience. The only people using three-dimensional mail were the occasional Luddite, collection agencies, agencies of power, and advertisers with their pervasive reams of rubbish.

Keagan removed his keys and opened the box. Low-resolution images of fruit, vegetables, toilet products, and candy, rained from the sullen metal box. The floor around Keagan's feet was instantly covered in vibrant, eye-scathing appeals to mastication. A slim letter in a bone-colored envelope lay amidst the pile of consumer catcalls. Keagan removed it, *SI Publishing* addressed to *Mr. S. Keagan.* "Looks serious. Why do I check the mail?" Keagan's time was up. He was closer to his page requirement than he had expected to be, but he needed another week to be sure. "I'll open it downstairs."

Keagan disappeared down the building's core staircase, he'd had enough of the wonky elevators. The ominous letter felt heavy—dense—in spite of being thin. That meant one thing: company letterhead—a heavier weight of paper for the officiality of it all. It was likely generated, signed, folded, shoved into a heavy envelope, and marked for delivery, by machines—which meant that someone had to do something unsavory and they preferred it to look administrative and not-personal. Keagan used a knife to open the envelope.

SI Publishing International | LLC, GmbH, MNE
5750 Wilshire Blvd. #3 Los Angeles, CA 90036-7201
International & Domestic Communications Division

Mr. Seward Keagan
548 S. Spring St.
Los Angeles, CA 90013
B-03
Revision Profile 455-75-93-NM13

Mr. Keagan:

This notice, pursuant to article Eleven (11), section f, sub section iii of the Author-Publisher Contract between S. Keagan (Author) and SI Publishing, LLC, GmbH, MNE (Publisher), signifies the Publisher's intent to terminate the aforementioned Author-Publisher Contract, in response to unacceptable activities on the part of the Author which compel the Publisher to nullify the Publisher's responsibility under article Eleven (11), section f, sub section iii of the Author-Publisher Contract. Thereby nullifying the aforementioned contract between the Author and the Publisher in toto immediately upon creation of this notice.

All contractual obligations regarding current, and past works by the Author are hereby rescinded. This decision is irrevocable and all encompassing.

Sincerely,
Jason P. Krause
Vice-President of Corporate Relationship Vectors
SouthWest Sub-region
International and Domestic Communications Division
SI Publishing International, LLC, GmbH, MNE

"I'm fucked." The thick letter fell to Keagan's feet. "Really fucked."

Without the Publisher, Keagan could conceivably spend his last days in the basement of the Spring Street Lofts, or worse, back in the drone hangar. He was in a Purgatorial bind: unable to leave the program without threat of imprisonment, and suddenly disqualified as a resident of Los Angeles. "Fuck, fuck, fuck." Keagan stood and crossed his studio to find his contract, "It's here... somewhere... where?...um..."

Keagan found the tobacco-stained pages bearing his four-year-old signature.

(11)...

(f)...

(iii) Should any (i.e. one (1), or more than one (1) simultaneously) of the above qualifications (Article 11, sections a - sub sections i and ii, b - sub section i, c - sub sections i - mxcix, d, e - sub sections i-iv, f, subsections i-iii) fail to be met to the satisfaction of the Publisher and/or any appointed Representative of the Publisher, the Contract will be terminated immediately by written notice.

Keagan sat silently for a very long time.

Outside in the still heat citizens walked their dogs, bragged about their team's victory, filed, and then collated hundreds of inane documents, and fielded thousands of mundane calls.

Keagan dressed, and when he finished, he checked his hair in the small over-the-sink mirror.

Keagan's walk down Wilshire Boulevard was mired in dry sunshine. Fifty-Seven Fifty Wilshire loomed in the near distance; Keagan watched the security shift change and slowly finished his cigarette before approaching building #3.

"Hello Bob," Keagan's eyes widened as he shouted his greeting to the daydreaming security guard.

"Hi Mr., wait, oh, shit, you're not supposed to be here," the front desk guard began to rise.

"Have a seat Bob, I am feeling particularly psychotic today and it's been a long time since I've hit anyone in the face. I'll only be a few minutes. Feel free to call the cops; I am not armed, it bears mentioning. To the cops. Please mention I am unarmed."

The security guard sat down and picked up the phone. He was neither scared nor angry; he simply shook his head in sympathy for the cracked author.

The receptionist at SI, on the other hand, recognized Keagan as soon as the elevator doors parted; she leapt into the air and tore off down a hallway screaming, "He's here!" to anyone within earshot.

"Where 'ya goin?" Keagan yelled casually. "I just want to talk to Jason," He lifted one of the expensive lobby chairs and hurled it over the receptionist's desk; the immense fake-slate water feature crowning the cavernous lobby seized and slowly wrested from it's mooring. Filthy, recycled water, ruddy with copper and ionization, fell as if freed from ancient floodgates onto the reception console, computer, and switchboard. Sparks flew in every direction and Keagan flinched backward.

"Fuck, didn't mean to do that."

Keagan strolled calmly down the hallway whistling *Fairytale In New York*.

"Mr. Keagan! Seward! How can I help you, my man?" Jason emerged from a fold in the corporate cubicles and rubbed his inevitably moist palms together nervously while straining to smile.

"Jason, yes, just the man I wanted to see. I got your letter."

"Oh? Welllll" Jason assessed his exits.

"No, no, don't worry, Jason. Let's go in here," Keagan motioned to an empty conference room overlooking the Fifty-Seven Fifty driveway and grounds.

Jason took a seat at the end of the table, as far from Keagan as he could without being too obvious about his terror.

"Jason, I want to know why. I came here today with the intention of beating someone to death, I will not tolerate lies. Are we clear?"

"We are, sir. Seward."

"This is the part where you tell me why I am suddenly unemployed."

"Yes, yes," Jason stammered, "I was asked to terminate your contract by our President of Distribution. Someone at the Connecticut office called in a personal order from Mr. Irvine that investment was to be shifted to Beihner."

"Who the fuck is Beihner?"

"Really? You haven't heard of..."

Keagan glared at him.

"...okay, Beihner is the *newest thing*. We fought for and won exclusive rights to his new series of novels involving a fatally charming, jet-setting vigilante who, as a side note *worth mentioning in the advertising* is prone to bouts of violent lycanthropy."

Keagan dropped his head. "Werewolves?"

"Precisely!" Jason beamed, and then remembered the gravity of his situation. "The vampire thing is dead, but the numbers show that werewolves haven't been admonished with the same passion as copycat sexy-vampire novels. Strangely, even vampire novels featuring werewolves are in decline, but werewolves by themselves, well, I think we have our billion-sale trifecta here."

"That's what you said about my..." Keagan rethought his comment. It was the sort of thing a cruelly jilted ex-lover would say. "All right. That explains it. See 'ya around Jason." Keagan stood and headed toward the conference room door. Employees that had been watching and eavesdropping on the other side of the glass walls evaporated as he approached.

Keagan left the building via emergency stairwell and headed down Wilshire with his head down and his eyes on the sidewalk.

As he hopped on his bus back downtown, a few cop cars skidded into place in front of the Fifty-Seven Fifty complex with their guns un-holstered. "A little late guys." Keagan muttered as he placed $2.50 into the bus' fare-sentinel.

When Keagan returned home several hours later with a BAC near .10 the building guard informed him that the police had stopped by.

The young man read from a note on his desk, "Detective Oliver Worecester would like to speak to you at your earliest convenience to clear everything up. 213-486-7000."

"It says *clear up*?" Keagan asked.

"It does." The guard answered after re-scanning the note.

"Thank you." He tucked the handwritten note into his jacket pocket and stumbled into the stairwell.

Keagan stared at his bland concrete wall. He needed something to happen. If he waited around for this Worecester guy to pay a visit he may end up occupying an even smaller cell. He needed to be on a plane to Dubai, or a slow boat to Argentina. If he stayed, he knew he would be wrapped up in whatever Worecester had cooking; for better or worse, once the authorities decide you are a *problem* the stigma never dies. There had to be a way; how did one disappear in these digital times?

The soft clack of rough soles against the marble stairs dripped slowly down Keagan's walls. For a moment he ignored them, preferring to concentrate on a *real* problem. Keagan considered for a moment that the hallucinations may be triggered in times of turmoil—the floor heaved. Keagan rushed to his feet, and threw open his door. Nothing. He rushed through the hall using his phone as a flashlight ready to maul the first shape that crossed his path. Still nothing. He ran back, retracing his steps, and again, before stopping.

Keagan heard the distant tinkling of a tiny bell. He had never heard a bell; what did that mean? To Keagan it sounded like a signal, was he being watched? He walked blindly toward the sound. He tried to peel the echo from the tomb's walls. As he walked past apartment B-09 he stopped. The air changed, subtly. He felt a soft wind brush his ankles.

The door was parted from the frame, a light was on inside, he could smell smoke again—this time he felt heat, bodies. This time, he would give into his madness, if for no other reason, to finally know that madness by name. Keagan heard soft shuffling as he pushed the door open and walked into the warm room, shutting the door behind him.

24

Cadence knocked once more.

"Come on Keagan, open the fucking door."

She knocked harder, "Keagan! What the fuck?"

Her last knock's echo faded and Cadence whispered to no one, "Please, Keagan. I think I miss you."

Socialist Dave entered the landing from the back stairwell. "Any luck?"

"No," Cadence straightened her back and turned, smiling, "the fucker's gone. We're out of here."

"We need to hit our posts. Good luck Cadence."

"Luck fucked me a long time ago."

Kuraš texted Cadence.

—*Do you see the black Crown Victoria parked on Sixth?*

Cadence responded.

—*Yes. I've seen that car before.*

—*It's been back and forth, parked all over the street for days. The cops aren't very smart, but they are watching the front door.*

—*Duly noted. Those morons chased me down once.*

—*When?*

—*Monday.*

—*They're here for you.*

—*Great, that's fucking perfect.*

—*Stay out of sight until I say otherwise. I have a feeling these idiots may come in handy if we need a diversion.*

—*10-4 Pops.*

ArtWalk—the downtown art sect's monthly mini-Mardi Gras—consumed Spring Street from Second to Ninth.

"It's too quiet, Koboko."

"Quiet? There are several thousand people on the streets Oliver, look around you. The City is alive and we are here staring at a door."

"You'd rather be frolicking with the hippies than tracking down a terrorist? You make me sick."

"Terrorist? Only if you consider birthday parties terror." Idi slapped his knee but his partner was unamused. "This is your shift, boss, and if you want to spend it on stakeout, I submit. Besides, can't beat the view, eh?"

Still nothing.

"Let's think about this, Oliver. If she's up to something, she's not going to run naked into the street with a knife. So why don't we agree to..."

The scanner leapt, "...disturbance, 245 in progress, 548 Spring. Corner of Sixth and Spring. Caucasian Female, dark hair, 5'6. Suspect last seen roaming naked down the hallways. Proceed with caution, suspect is armed."

Cadence texted Kuraš.

—*The piggies are on the move.*

—*We need more time.*

—*You don't have it. Something spooked them. They're headed toward the front door right now. I met one of these guys at Hank's. His name's Oliver, and he's a fragile flower.*

Kuraš called the front desk.

"Hello? Yes, I believe so. Hold on," the Spring Street Lofts' front desk guard cupped his hand over the receiver and called, "Are the pathetic, monosyllabic primates, otherwise known as the LAPD in attendance?" The guard had great difficulty holding back his laughter during his recital.

Worecester and Koboko stopped and looked at one another before turning and walking menacingly toward the front desk. The guard tossed the phone to the rapidly advancing officers. Worecester caught the receiver, "Who the fuck is this?"

"I'm the one you morons didn't know you were looking for. You should have taken my entire operation down a long, long time ago. How does it feel to be such dense assholes?" Kuraš' voice smiled on the other side of the line.

Worecester silently turned crimson, and his knuckles blurred white with rage.

"That wasn't a rhetorical question." Kuraš broke the silence. "You are even more mentally handicapped in person than I expected. And let me assure you, I had a gratuitously low opinion of you to begin with."

"That's it. Where are you, punk?"

"Punk? I'm old enough to be your father. I'm either in Puerto Vallarta or I'm on the twelfth floor. I'd check both, but not necessarily in that order."

"He's on twelve" Worecester shouted to Koboko. "Let's go."

Koboko wedged his arm into a closing elevator, and the two men rushed skyward as they inspected their weapons. The digital number seven on the elevator wall changed to eight, and the elevator heaved to a stop. Worecester and Koboko lost their footing and hit the ground hard.

"I swear I'm going to kill every one of these motherfuckers."

"We're between eight and nine." Worecester reached his fingers between the inner doors. "I can boost you up to the outer doors, you should be able to push through."

The long hallways were blackened; no sound betrayed the cavern beyond the consuming veil of darkness. Worecester and Koboko took out their weapons and slowly walked into the hallway crisscrossing their flashlight beams as they cleared the hall foot by foot.

"There's an open door. There."

"Approach slowly, standard procedure from here on out Koboko."

"I know that Oliver."

Candles consumed the floor of the loft and gave a low fog of light.

Worecester covered his nose. "It smells like shit in here."

"I'm checking behind that curtain. Watch my back." Koboko pressed himself against the wall and slowly moved a curtain draped over a doorway.

Oliver continued looking around the apartment. Everything was in place; there was no sign of a disturbance or struggle.

Koboko called out weakly from the room. "Oliver..."

Worecester rushed past the curtain and raised his pistol.

"Put it away Oliver. They're dead."

"Jesus Christ." Worecester backed away. Four corpses lay blank-eyed in a hurried pile just beyond his feet. A thin night screen made of paper separated the unblinking bodies from the bed.

"This doesn't seem like our punk rock kid," Koboko shined his light around the room.

A plea gurgled from one of the corpse's lips. "Pllllease. I'm n-not dead."

Koboko held the man's head, "Who did this to you?"

"I did." Lara cast a frail shadow on the bed behind the detectives. Her naked flesh was luminous; old scars and fresh gashes consumed her arms and legs. Both detectives stared, transfixed until she approached.

"Wait! Stop right there."

"What's wrong, boys? Am I not pretty enough for you?"

"Don't take another step. This man needs a doctor, and by the look of things, so do you. Why don't you slip a robe on, sweetie, and we can talk about this in the car ..."

Lara plunged a wide knife into Worecester's throat. "No. No. No! It isn't supposed to be like this. He has to watch."

Idi pulled his pistol from its holster. "You need to put that knife down. Right now!"

"But I didn't do this. I couldn't hurt anyone." She pressed her forehead against the barrel of his gun.

The detective felt the prick of a needle as she suddenly gripped his waist. He missed his only clear shot, and was soon clawing at the floor and firing into the ceiling.

Lara stretched out on the edge of the bed and watched the detective convulse. She smiled at Jean-Baptisté. "I'm sorry that we suffered this disturbance my love. The detective will be ready soon."

§

Socialist Dave and Cadence were long gone now. Kuraš rushed down a forgotten staircase, through a retail access corridor, and emerged on Sixth Street as four armored vehicles and eleven squad cars descended on the entrance to the Spring Street Lofts—screeching, sliding, and generally making a further nuisance of themselves.

When he reached Ejido Eréndira, a new sun was rising.

ANCILLARY PATHS

THE OUTRAGEOUS AND UNFORTUNATE CONSEQUENCES OF DECONSTRUCTION

At certain times in history, a certain *something* happens; something that no one, but no one, sees coming. It used to be called *irony*, but by the time the intellectuals of the Nineteen-Nineties were cast aside (or cast themselves aside) *irony* came to mean nothing more than the opposite of *wrinkly*.

American thought became a projected, singular force, like the East Australian Current—all who approached were drug forcibly into monosyllabic slumber, and relaxed into ignorance like a drunk in a cheap evening gown. Yet, it was under these conditions that the American people were introduced to Derrida Aloysius. By deign of marriage (the Groom's fifth, the Bride's second) Derrida became tertiary cousins with a well-connected lawyer in Los Angeles. This distant American relative found his Spanish cousin's quaint postcards and letters from the Basque countryside quite charming in a docu-drama, *country mouse vs. city mouse* sort of way. He sent word to his cousin that he was welcome at his home in the hills above Los Angeles at any time.

Derrida received his cousin's offer and arrived at LAX in three week's time. He could not fathom bothering his cousin, so Derrida set out on foot in search of a distant place called *Beverly Hills* and a bent canyon lane called *Summer Holly Circle*. The chaos of Century Boulevard numbed Derrida more than the cold. Derrida sat on a bus bench near a Motel 6 on Century Boulevard and lit a hand-rolled cigarette. He had a sturdy 21-22 kilometer journey ahead, much of which, unbeknownst to Derrida would be treacherous and steep indeed. A battered car slowly rolled to a stop in front of Derrida's bench as he quietly studied his map and smoked. Derrida ignored the automobile as its passengers exited their respective doors.

"Hey, partner, what's going on tonight?" A man in a plain black uniform with no official markings asked as he tucked a long baton into his belt.

Derrida looked up from his map, "I apologize, my English is not as good as.-"

"Stand up. Now."

Derrida waited, he did not understand why the man was asking him to stand. "Does this mean something in America?"

"That's it." The younger uniformed man struck Derrida on the head and sent him to the concrete reeling. When Derrida awoke he was in a caged seat in the back of a car and the two uniformed men were driving down an immense roadway with endless planes of asphalt crisscrossing in the sky.

"Where are you taking me, please?" Derrida asked.

"Oh now you speak-a da en-glaze, huh?" The uniformed men laughed. "Fuck you, you're going downtown."

Derrida waited patiently. They approached an immense cluster of tall buildings rife with reflecting eyes. As they passed through the tangled web of on- and off-ramps to something called "Interstate 10 - Santa Monica Freeway" the uniformed men pressed between the immense skyscrapers and night became illuminated in dirty yellow light and blinding fluorescent markets and bars. The streets were littered with the inebriated and the cast-aside alike, blending into a single stream of noise and personal-agenda that echoed off every stone, brick, and tile surface blindly.

The cacophony peeled away as they left the skyscrapers behind. The streets became narrow, dark, and spotted by bright tents pitched directly on the sidewalks. Masses of human bodies moved slowly like flocks of narcotized birds, trying to escape, and making it only a step— or flap—at a time. The uniformed men pulled to a slow stop near a fenced park. Men and women milled around aimlessly inside the iron barrier. When the automobile's doors opened, the cowed people in the park stopped instantly and turned their heads in unison.

One of the uniformed men stood next to the car and fired a shotgun into the air, "Any of you fucking freaks makes a move, and I'll mow you down one by one."

The younger officer opened Derrida's door and pulled him out. "We're going to leave the zip-ties on, more fun that way." With a boot to the pants-seat, he sent Derrida head first into the crowd of vacant, diminished, monoliths. "If you're lucky the immigration round up will find you in the morning and deport you. Until then, welcome to Skid Row."

The uniformed men shot two or three curious bystanders in the extremities for being too close. Several crowds of people began to move toward the car and the two men hastily shut their doors and sped in their anonymous black car toward friendlier climes.

Derrida looked up into the crowd of people. Some wore hospital gowns with fuzzy boots, some scarves, jackets, piece-meal dresses, slacks, old suits, and several *D.A.R.E.* and *Los Angeles Women's Shelter* windbreakers. All had been on these streets for longer than Derrida cared to imagine.

"Look at you." One man spoke instead of staring. "Just dropped off here like garbage. Well, welcome to the dump young man, I'm Stanley."

"Kaixo Stanley," Derrida took his hand. "Non nago? Sorry, where am I?"

"Skid Row, baby. Downtown Los Angeles, where they dump everyone at one time or another."

"Dump?"

"Yeah." Stanley smiled and extended his hand.

"Ah, thank you," Derrida smiled warmly.

"Dump, as in, drive up and boot out, as you have recently witnessed."

"Why?"

"Let me guess. They found you sitting somewhere, *inconvenient*, you didn't speak perfect English, didn't have papers, no job, no dinero, am I close?"

"Perfecto."

"Those assholes were Neighborhood Ambassadors. Picked you up at LAX, right?"

"Correct. I just landed this evening."

"They can't have indigent illegals wandering around on Century Boulevard. It's bad for tourism."

"Illegals?"

"You. Illegal. You weren't born here and can't prove you have permission to be here, so..."

"Oh. Is it that strict? I thou---"

"You thought what most people think. Problem is, shit ain't true. Anyway, you're on Incorporated Skid Row, the only place in LA you can pitch a tent over night. The City likes to keep its homelessness in one area. You were dropped here because calling the police these days is like requesting a Secret Service escort," Stanley laughed.

"I need to get to Summer Holly Circle in Beverly Hills."

"Don't we all."

"Can you show me the way?"

"Sure. You don't want to head out tonight. You'll be pushing it to catch the last trains into Hollywood."

"I have to try."

"Okay, a few blocks over is fifth, hang left, walk toward the buildings. At Hill you'll see the subway entrance, you want to go to 'North Hollywood.'" Stanley turned abruptly and shouted, "Franklin. Franklin, get your ass over here." Franklin complied warily. "Come here punk, show me that knife."

Franklin pulled a long, straight blade from beneath his limp poncho. Stanley swiped it from his hand effortlessly. "Who has your blade now?" Stanley taunted the visibly agitated transient.

Stanley slipped the blade between the zip-ties and freed Derrida's wrists.

"Thank you Stanley, I am in your debt."

"I don't believe in debt friend, part of why I'm down here. Ride the Red Line until you get to Hollywood and Highland. Get off. South on Highland to Sunset, west on Sunset. Sunset goes to Beverly Hills, you can't miss it, big ass signs and everything. You'll have to ask about the details when you get there."

Derrida headed between the haphazard minefield of tents, boxes, legs, arms, and offers of sexual and/or medicinal gratification—real cheap—right now. By the time he approached Spring Street the faces had changed; plump collegiate seraphs sucked on pints and engaged in banal conversation on every corner.

The immense metal chasm leading below the street to the subway platform was overwhelming. Derrida was dazzled as he descended the endless waterfall of escalators. Rows of television sets mounted to the ceiling were blank and the platform was silent. Derrida set his pack on a bench and soon fell into a deep and tumultuous sleep.

When Derrida woke two men were standing above him.

"Are you alright sir?" One of the men asked.

"Yes..." Derrida's eyes focused, both men were dressed in black with utility belts and tall, menacing boots. These men were alight with metal medallions and identification badges—LAPD.

"You can't sleep down here, the station has been closed for an hour now, you need to move along."

"But sir, I have no place to go. I have just arrived and I am trying to reach my cousin's home in Beverly Hills. His name is-"

"Look, I don't give a fuck if you're hunting for Snoopy and Woodstock's house, get the fuck up."

"Sir..."

"We're going to have to take this one to Skid Row." The Sergeant added from behind the more combative junior officer.

"Please, I have just come from there. I landed at the airport and two men in uniforms hit me and drove me to this Skid Row and left me. I am not an *illegal*, I have simply lost my way."

The officer had heard enough, "Illegal eh?" He pulled Derrida's hands behind his back and had them zip-tied with rodeo-rider speed. Derrida was startled; authority figures in America moved so rapidly to incapacitate a calm individual. It was as if they had received special and diligent training, orders to incapacitate in all situations. Derrida remembered that he was in America, home of the legal (and illegal) handgun; these officers had likely been shot at or knew officers who had. Derrida tried to have sympathy for their potential fear.

"Sir, this one has already been cuffed tonight." The younger officer inspected Derrida's split zip-ties.

"I am not dangerous officers, I am only waiting for a train to North Hollywood."

"Thought you were going to Beverly Hills," The Sergeant's grey eyes narrowed.

"I am. Is there a more direct route? I am at your mercy, I am lost."

"I don't know how direct it is, but you're going to spend the night downtown and we'll see what's up in the morning, okay?" The calmer officer spoke again.

"Please, gentlemen, I will leave." Derrida bent his head in submission.

"You had your chance," the combative cop rushed Derrida and pushed him along the concrete platform, "you heard the Sergeant, you're coming with us."

Derrida was stripped and roughly searched upon entering the booking facility. He spent two nights in a cell before an officer in a civilian suit approached him.

"We're going to process you along with all of the other hippies. Let's go."

"Hippies?"

Derrida was not answered. He was walked to a long, armored school bus, shoved into a seat, and restrained. The bus was filled with people who had been chained to benches for hours. Most had taken the humiliating liberty of relieving themselves on the floors of the long clanking dungeon. The officers driving the vehicle played xmas carols at ear-shattering volumes and closed a sound-depressing gate between the cockpit and the prisoners.

By the time Derrida saw the inside of a jail cell, the sun was rising over Union Station. His DNA was collected, and they shuffled him into a manufactured category of "failure to disperse"—a misdemeanor—that warranted a five thousand US-Dollar bail. Needless to say, Derrida was at a loss and had only his cousin's address, no phone number.

Members of the Lawyer's Guild offered to help him post bail, but he refused humbly. "I will await trial, I have done nothing wrong." Derrida was granted his wish and he spent three weeks among those swept up that night in what they called an *Eviction*. Persons swept up with poor reason and at times for no reason at all.

Derrida was surprised to hear that American police had resorted to such extreme tactics, but he was beginning to understand that America was numb to extremes. His cellmates told him about the first Occupy Wall Street protest, how it had been far more massive than anyone imagined it could be. The violent treatment of protestors had sparked a firestorm and the protest became a permanent occupation of Zuccotti Park. From there, Occupations sprung up nation-wide and in several foreign countries.

Derrida's trial was short and sweet; he was ordered to leave the United States *at once* or face deportation and detention. Derrida pleaded with the authorities but it only seemed to infuriate them, so he ceased. He was accused of belonging to an anti-government group called *Occupy Los Angeles*.

"You will be released, but your continued presence in the United States is grounds for permanent detention. Do you understand?"

"I do."

"You may leave."

Derrida took the desk Sergeant's bus token and rode back to the Pershing Square Station.

"Al?" Derrida's cousin opened the large oak door to his canyonside home. "Is that you? You look like shit, come in, come in." Mr. Baudron ushered Derrida into his large, warm home. "I got your letter, when did you arrive?"

"It's not important, I am here, thank you for your hospitality. I am in your debt."

"Nonsense, we are family now. No?"

"We are. Thank you." Derrida placed his sodden backpack on the ground and collapsed into a large chair.

When Derrida woke he was swaddled in impossibly soft comforters plump with down and lined in silk. He could not recall moving, or being moved from the large chair in the foyer. He was happy to be alive and in his cousin's care.

At a quiet, candle-lit dinner Mr. Baudron asked Derrida what happened to him.

"I am not sure, I arrived several weeks ago and as I sat smoking a cigarette two men approached me and threw me into a black vehicle."

"Police?" Mrs. Baudron asked.

"No, Neighborhood Ambassador, I was told. They dumped me in a place called Skid Row. I tried to make the last train to North Hollywood and the Policia found me sleeping in the station. I was put into a large bus with protestors of some sort, at City Hall"

"The Occupiers," Mr. Baudron interrupted.

"Bai, something like that. I was detained in the bus, prisoners were forced to urinate and defecate on themselves. Our zip-ties were far too tight. We were treated like animals. Some of the officers were embarrassed and offered us pastries and coffee when we arrived at the booking station, but they were soon replaced by prison guards."

"Why would they think you were an Occupier?"

"I can't say, for the most part I thought I was just on my way to being deported. They collected my DNA and processed my information, I was confined to a cell for three weeks before being informed by a judge that I was a member of an 'anti-government group' and that I was ordered to leave the US immediately."

Mrs. Baudron looked at Mr. Baudron, "Darling, are you thinking..."

"Yes my love, yes I am."

"Derrida, would you be able to tell that story in a courtroom?" Mrs. Baudron asked sympathetically, leadingly.

"Of course, every day for the rest of my life if necessary."

"Perfect." Mr. Baudron smiled broadly and gestured to his wife, "Honey, make a call to Celia will you? I need to see her husband immediately."

Mr. and Mrs. Baudron held a press conference and announced their intention to sue the City of Los Angeles for their treatment of a legally visiting Spanish citizen during the first Eviction. The City, the LAPD, and the Xenon Private Security firm were scandalized internationally and pleaded, on bended knee, to pay a hefty compensatory sum to Mr. Derrida Aloyisius for his pain and anguish. Mr. and Mrs. Baudron celebrated and rode their newly minted wave of upgraded social power until it subsided.

Derrida had other plans; he spent a formidable number of hours studying American jurisprudence while completing his immigration process. He began crisscrossing the county on bicycle, train, and bus, attending local, city, county, and state hearings. As the name Derrida Aloyisius faded into the American Media dustbin, Aloyisius 'Al' Baudron wrangled his way (with Mr. Baudron's solemn and discreet financial patronage) onto the Beverly Hills City Council.

His motivations remained hidden and his career seemed boring, dispassionate, and technical. No council members feared his rational voting pattern and he was a dependable vote for reason when necessary. When an issue was unreasonable, frivolous, passion-fueled, or under-researched, he could be counted on to abstain in protest. Under his cousin's tutelage, Aloyisius shook hands with the proper pillars of polite society and walked humbly into the invisible halls of power.

With each committee chairmanship, each public works project that finished, astonishingly, on time, with each quiet term of service in the various regions of municipal influence, Aloyisius became a silent player in the intimate business of the city that wished him detained, deported, and demoralized so few years ago.

Aloyisius received accolades from the Governor of California just prior to announcing his bid for the Mayor's office. No one questioned that Aloyisius would take the prestigious office. The sordid truth was clear to all, Aloyisius did not earn the office; without his cousin's substantial ties and access to media outlets, the Baudron campaign could only have failed.

Mr. Baudron paraded around with his *Dear cousin* showing him off as the *son he should have had*, a brooch of potential power. "Al understands the common man, but he is crystal-clear when it comes to the *un*common man."

Aloyisius melted into the Office of Mayor. His shy, reserved, and private demeanor made him mysterious to a city constantly bombarded by celebrity authority. The people forgot that their Mayor existed. His influence was too subdued: things cost less, the roads were cleaner and more often repaired on time, the dog-eat-dog barbarity of the city seemed, for a time, to calm.

During his third year in office, Aloyisius unveiled a clandestine plan to minimize government spending and reward jurisdiction over most of the City's business to the people.

"The time of hierarchal administration is long past. This City is what it is because of the citizens that call it home. It has nothing to do with me, and it has nothing to do with the Chief of Police or the City Councils. Los Angeles, I am giving your city back."

Over the next three hundred forty-eight days Aloyisius triggered legislative directives he had been amassing while managing the various tiers of the City's organs—hierarchal frames are most vulnerable to their own strictures. By edict, by order, and by law, Aloyisius dismantled the City's government and placed the potency of execution in the hands of the managerial and working classes by virtue of public and open hearings, legislative paralysis without consent, and equal public campaign financing—private money was no longer invited. The sitting heads of the City Councils, under the strict guidance of the Chief of Police, ordered the Mayor to cease and to resign. Aloyisius ignored his subordinates' mutiny and continued with his work.

The Board of Education stepped forward in a show of faith and within three months, School District Superintendency became a discontinued practice. LAUSD stripped the City's hierarchy placing Principals at the helm, and Principals at the mercy of their students' parents. The Departments of Transportation, Building Services, Street Services, and Waste Removal attempted to follow suit but were stopped dead by a court injunction.

Federal forces arrived en masse at 200 North Spring Street on the afternoon of January 21st and surrounded City Hall. Sympathetic LAFD battalions gathered on the steps of all cardinal points and refused to allow Federal forces into City Hall. Requests from embattled and anxious Chiefs helped curb revolt and insurrection as nearly two million people ebbed and flowed into the city during the terse eleven-day standoff.

By fiat, Aloyisius dissolved the office of Mayor of the City of Los Angeles from deep within City Hall. With an odd and penetrating smile, he walked slowly down the west steps and quietly asked the protective ring of LAFD to pardon him as he passed. He thanked each of them in turn, and walked into Federal custody exhausted and relieved.

Aloyisius' initial *troubles* in the United States were grounds for his immediate deportation. Savvy men in business suits with non-descript badges in their jacket pockets took interest in his former nomen, "Why the name change, Derrida?"

"It seemed appropriate, my cousin thought his name made for a strong candidate. Besides, Jacques Derrida is a...well, you know."

"No I don't. What I know is that you were rounded up in the first Eviction downtown, right?"

"Yes, but it as a mistake. You see, I was picked up by a team of private security guards and dropped in Skid Row..."

"That doesn't interest me. Captain?" A police officer in a wrinkled brown suit entered the interrogation room. "Wrap him up. What we have here is a co-conspirator from a foreign country. One that received preferential treatment and ended up committing an act of terrorism after gaining political office; we're making an example of him."

"Yes sir, we're on it."

"What's happening?" Derrida asked quietly.

"You're affiliated with a known terrorist organization. You're an anarchist, and anti-American, and now you're going to be the high profile collar that gets me the fuck out of this hellhole."

"I don't understand."

"Welcome to America. Sit back and enjoy the ride."

ADVERT-FLAGE — AD8.0

A century ago, the bastions of corporate power created the modern advertising environment. Through the revolutionary crisis control techniques of Bernays and Lee, the Robber Barons learned that slick sleight of hand effectively whitewashed their crimes. By sinking millions (eventually billions) into the burgeoning *advertising* industry they set out to systematically violate each and every human being on the planet from the comfort of their own home.

The problem has always been that you cannot prove a 1:1 relationship between the ad campaign and the negative or positive results. Though firms have spent the better part of that century devising complex lexicons and explanations, it is still impossible to say, accurately that 'this spot caused *this* sale'—spot:sale.

As a result of this empirical dishonesty, the beast evolved to make broader, more abstract claims about it's necessity to business, which created a swindled, snake-oil slush-pot absorbing filthy lucre and transforming it into *internet presence, public relations,* and *campaign contributions*. The money changed hands, was held and fawned over by the advertising conglomerates, and then set free to crawl back into the coffers of those from whose nest it originally fell. Rinse. Repeat.

In the late 10s Pre-New Millennium (pNM), a crisis of existential proportions shook the tentacled foundations of the *International United Markets* advertising cabal. Fair-haired great-great-grandsons that slipped from the bowels of Harvard, NYU, USC, UCLA, and Yale withered in the shade of fetid degrees in Public and Privileged Communications. Their fathers watched the unsteady, and at times, fatal rise and fall of advertising through the final decades of the Lost Millennium. Corporate-Social coercion had tiptoed through revolutions, ideological struggles, wars, famine, and widespread death to masticate parasitically on the flesh of every (all too) willing consumer.

Handmade Print advertising (Ad1.0) was widely accepted throughout the community as Advertising's genesis. Mass production (Ad2.0) brought Ad1.0 to every living human creature—whether they liked it or not—and with the invention of radio (Ad3.0) and later television (Ad4.0) advertising mastered the arts of infiltration, subliminal innuendo, and saturation. The American government worked tirelessly to secure control over the content transmitted over the original radio and television channels; blasphemy, decadence, and debauchery remained the purview of Hollywood films until Cable (Ad5.0) crashed the stuffy soirée.

The rise of the personal computer destroyed the static nature of advertising. CD-ROM Interactive advertisements (Ad6.0), portfolios on the fly, and the adjoining product pimping, gave the world a surface-level glance at a human existence experienced completely through computers. When the early connections that finally formed the *World Wide Web* (Ad7.0) flickered into existence, the United States gave the world its final and desperate wish: *to do all things from the comfort, safety, and anonymity of* home. Misanthropy by modem.

By year 13 of the New Millennium (NM), Ad7.0 had stagnated. New generations of consumers learned to parry in/direct marketing expertly as soon as they learned to use a computer. The fair-haired great-great-grandsons needed more; in their ancestor's time, advertising had always been a *gentleman's* game, where results could be abstract and carry the weight of precise science. The game had run its course; consumers felt compelled only by their subjective interests, collective-coercion seemed fated to go the way of the Bubal Hartebeest.

In 16 NM the fair-haired great-great-grandsons' asses were collectively saved by a renegade art movement that blossomed in fertile north Georgia soil. Several graduate students began producing small-scale campaigns nailed to wooden light poles near the University of Georgia.

Their technique was to engage, rather than pontificate, to allure, rather than inform. The dogmatic advertising tenets of the late Nineteenth Century, Twentieth Century, and early Twenty-First Century were discarded. Using product/service/company name/logo as often as possible, was abandoned for an aesthetic sense of information- and structural-minimalism.

Sweeping, dramatic colors, densely abstract references, coded URLs and innuendo, were used to attract the subject's attention and compel them to further investigate. Relevance was placed back on participation rather than inundation and the radical students' camouflaged advertisements were compelling even if the products they lead to were not. (A point driven home by a South Carolina group sympathetic to the movement that branched into a process leading consumers to something extremely disagreeable. They considered it a sort of tough-love approach, a hard and permanent reminder that the joy was in the choice, not in consumption.)

A young man by the infamous surname, Krauthammer, was placed in a cell overnight near Chapel Hill, North Carolina after an alleged (and later confirmed, but hastily dismissed) sexual assault. Krauthammer was terrified. He gravitated to a young Caucasian man who sat silently on the corner of the small town's holding cell. The young man was dressed in black and had a quiet calm to his visage.

"Any chance we're getting out tonight?" Krauthammer asked shyly.

"None." The young man answered matter-of-factly.

"What are you in for?"

"Vandalism."

"Really?"

"Yes."

"Seems a bit harsh. What did you vandalize?"

"A billboard."

"They think I raped a girl. Me." Krauthammer feigned indignation. "Can you believe it?"

The young man was silent.

"So, why the billboard?"

"Advert-Flage."

"Okay. And that is?"

"Camouflaged advertising."

"I've never heard of it."

"Better that way."

Krauthammer looked around and tried once more, "Look, tell me all about it, I have nothing but time kid."

The young man gave a passionless dissertation on the Advert-Flage movement, but could not hide his glee when he described his elaborate piece of *vandalism* and the message waiting for brave adventurers who accepted the challenge.

"So the point is to obscure the message? Beyond any feasible brand-recognition?" Krauthammer asked.

"Fuck the brand." The young man smiled wearily. "That concept of advertising is long dead anyway."

Krauthammer smiled. "Thank you young man. What's your name?"

"Doesn't matter, Pops."

Krauthammer smiled again. *These miscreants may have accidentally invented the newest iteration of advertising.* He felt no ethical or social obligation to the lower-class, nameless man. "Is anonymity a part of the movement, or personal?"

"Personal. I plan on making tracks for the west coast as soon as they let me out. Besides, I find people particularly unpleasant in the long term. No offense."

"None taken." Krauthammer smiled and turned to the sun as it set over the forest-choked western horizon.

Henish, Kallisti, Bricoler & Sireikol Group (HKB&SG) welcomed Krauthammer back with open arms. Upon hearing his revolutionary plan to subvert the dominant advertising paradigm, they sequestered him to an undisclosed location where he spent the rest of his days as the reclusive and undeservedly pampered weak link in a global cabal. Krauthammer, like all revolutionary catalysts, had to be kept from the public eye—for his own safety, and for the safety of the notion that HKB&SG created Ad8.0 within its ranks and with good old-fashioned underemployed American grey matter.

HKB&SG ran with Advert-Flage, first by converting to the more market-friendly and monopolistic *Camo-Tising* and *Camo-Vert*, then by publishing a paper entitled *Reawakening the Slumbering Consumer Beast* which laid out the principles that 1) consumers who are required to be *involved* tend to feel more compelled to purchase, and that 2) the all-correcting Free Market had really, all along—*wink wink*—been based more on allure than on information. The religiously held notion that teasing in the digital age equaled suicide was challenged soundly. The paper was published under the name of a Yale economic group and rapidly became the banner under which Advertising, like so many art forms before it, endeavored to remain relevant by becoming ever more vague.

Cable, radio, and print ads were stripped of product references, product logos, and brands. All attendant copy (if the Traditionalists had to be placated) was required to avoid referring to the product, provider of the product, or the service the product provided—at all costs. Clickable links led to elaborate websites and pipelines to product interfaces and complicated virtual shopping carts, ever seeking to keep the consumer salivating in anticipation—just a little longer. Dandelion- and kudzu-polluted highway shoulders became cramped with high-resolution billboards of swirling colors, blatantly non sequitur visuals and neural sleights-of-hand.

HKB&SG unveiled their "Revolutionary new way to increase revenue."[1] For a time, albeit brief on the scale of human events, HKB&SG pimped Ad8.0 successfully. Just long enough, it bears mentioning, for every lesser firm from sea to shining sea to mimic HKB&SG and ultimately return advertising to a state of banal status quo conformity.

The purposely-vague imagery of Ad8.0 allowed vandalism and graffiti to go mostly unnoticed to product-hungry consumer-detectives. Subtle, alterations made under the cover of darkness remained unseen by the general public and by the advertisers—who were ostensibly footing the bill to deliver the covert, coded messages.

By the time the young vandal from the jail reached practiced adult apathy, and long after Krauthammer's obsidian heart ceased to beat, underground anti-authoritarian groups ranging from Occupy Los Angeles to local street gangs began using the neglected highway beacons to transmit coded messages to sympathizers, rivals, and fellow revolutionaries. The Insurrection Protection Act, responsible for codifying the Department of Justice's listing of six-hundred eighty four organizations as *terrorist*, included a closed-Committee amendment ordering law enforcement officials to *dismantle, destroy, and repurpose all advertising surfaces and practices known to the Department of Justice, the Central Intelligence Agency, and the Federal Bureau of Investigation as the primary vehicle of choice for underground insurrectionist movements and their associated communiqués.*

---

[1]   A claim that was later dropped from all corporate copy after subsequent lawsuits terminated in the Ninth Circuit of Appeals and required the firm to add a footnote to all publications—*the Parent Company a) in no way advocates for, or calls upon, or refers to, 'revolution' in a positive political context, that b) 'new' in this context did not actually mean 'new;' rather it meant the more diminished 'semi-, faux- or structurally-new,' within verifiable reason, i.e. more than fifty-one percent of the process had been altered, and that c) the aforementioned 'new revenue' was not a demonstrable effect; rather, it was a hoped-for or desired-greatly effect that HKB&SG insists is at least .006% feasible.

3-15-18NM — NEVIS PEAK

Cadence,

I hope you are well, wherever you ended up. Where I ended up, it's balmy and the insects are more peer than parasite. The sun melts into a vast sea, unsullied by landlocked distortion, and beauty is based on comfort rather than critique.

I hope this finds Kuraš, Dave, and you, safely removed from what—I was informed—was a very thorough raid on the Building. No one saw you escape, and no one saw you taken into custody. I'll comfort myself with the notion that if you are reading this, you are at least alive.

Same here. Alive, that is. You could say I caught the last train out of Los Angeles and decided not to stop after my hosts went their separate ways. I stayed in safe, northerner-weary tourist traps and then moved south to Puerto Vallarta. The death march through Mexico City and on to Cancun was perilous.

I remained in the Lesser Antilles archipelago and settled my lot with refugee and revolutionary communities occupying an American Veterinary University. In searching for an alternative, I was forced to come to terms with the state of the world—there's just nowhere to go anymore, to escape. War is everywhere, and no one is safe from the United States.

I miss you all. Strange as that may seem to both of us. I have also had a change of heart. I lie awake at night thinking about you, and your son, Kuraš, and Dave. I think about bringing you all here, and I know I cannot feel complete without *trying. There is a place for all of you here. This is a safe place, for now. Safe from the president's bombs.*

Someone is watching you. If you cannot come, then do nothing. Leave this letter on your table and it will be properly destroyed. If you will come, raise your left hand to your right shoulder, brush three times, and then place it over your fork. It is of the utmost importance that this seems natural. We will not be the only ones watching. I have arranged for safe passage and you will be in very capable hands throughout.

I do hope to see you as soon as humanly possible. If this is au revoir, however, be safe and be free. Never settle for one over the other.

Yours indeed,
Seward Keagan

Acknowledgements

Thank you to Spaceboy for being the kind of press where a book like this feels comfortable. Thanks to Nate Ragolia and Shaunn Grulkowski for their vision, tenacity, and generosity. A deep well of respect for my family and their infinite patience - yes, daddy is still staring at the same group of words. Thanks to Dave Alston and Meg Teske for being down there, during everything that followed. Love and respect to Saskia and David; we miss you. Many thanks to Jordan Rothacker for his eyes, ears, and insight. Immense gratitude and respect to James Baldwin, Noam Chomsky, and Howard Zinn for spreading sanity in an insane nation, and to Emma Goldman and Rudolf Rocker for giving beautiful ideas practical structure. Finally, very special thanks to the Congressional Research Service for their 2011 publication *Instances of Use of United States Armed Forces Abroad, 1798-2010*. An eye opening document indeed; alarming that it is not required reading in elementary schools.

About the Author

William was much younger when he wrote this book. Since then, he's written a few more books, published enough short stories to avoid listing them all here, and proudly served as the managing editor for Black Hill Press and 1888. He knows that tyranny is not immortal, but William is an old guy now, and it's only gotten worse.

About the Publishing Team

Nate Ragolia was labeled as "weird" early in elementary school, and it stuck. He's a lifelong lover of science fiction, and a nerd/geek. In 2015 his first book, *There You Feel Free*, was published by 1888's Black Hill Press. He's also the author of *The Retroactivist*, published by Spaceboy Books. He founded and edits BONED, an online literary magazine, has created webcomics, and writes whenever he's not playing video games or petting dogs.

Shaunn Grulkowski has been compared to Warren Ellis and Phillip K. Dick and was once described as what a baby conceived by Kurt Vonnegut and Margaret Atwood would turn out to be. He's at least the fifth best Slavic-Latino-American sci-fi writer in the Baltimore metro area. He's the author of *Retcontinuum*, and the editor of *A Stalled Ox* and *The Goldfish*, among others.

www.ingramcontent.com/pod-product-compliance
Lightning Source LLC
Chambersburg PA
CBHW032005170626
46807CB00006B/2657

* 9 7 8 1 9 5 1 3 9 3 0 3 8 *